"I wasn't expecting...this."

Mal sounded perturbed. "This... chemistry between us can't interfere with the race."

"It won't," Abbie replied in a brisk tone, despite the fact his kiss had practically melted her spine! Her story had to come first, no matter how attracted she might be to her subject.

"No touching if we can possibly avoid it."

"And no more kissing," she put in firmly.

Mal gazed at her mouth. "Yes, no kissing under any circumstances," he said hoarsely.

Then Abbie suddenly remembered. "But what about Roxanne?"

With Roxanne in the picture, she and Mal would have to pretend to be lovers up to the time they started the race. By then, surely, they'd never be capable of just switching off their emotions....

LYNN TURNER is a going concern. In addition to keeping house for her husband and two sons, she teaches creative writing and works as a remedial reading instructor in Indiana. And on top of that, she writes and still finds time to dabble with oil paints and sew occasionally. How does she do it? She says she has a button that reads: The only thing domestic about me is that I was born in this country. Oh, well...Lynn's dubious attitude to housework is readily made up for by her storytelling talent.

Books by Lynn Turner

LYNN TURNER

impulsive gamble

Harlequin Books

TORONTO • NEW YORK • LONDON
AMSTERDAM • PARIS • SYDNEY • HAMBURG
STOCKHOLM • ATHENS • TOKYO • MILAN

Harlequin Presents first edition September 1989
ISBN 0-373-11205-X

Original hardcover edition published in 1988
by Mills & Boon Limited

CHAPTER ONE

'Y'KNOW what I'm wonderin?'

The seemingly idle question was delivered in a drawl as slow and thick as molasses. In comparison, the answer sounded terse, a bit impatient.

'No, and to tell the truth, I don't much care.'

The second man's drawl wasn't as pronounced, but it was there, softening and blurring his deep, rumbling voice so that it made Abbie think of warm, golden honey.

'I'm wonderin' how you've managed to live to the ripe old age of thirty-six, when it's a well-known fact that you've been brain-dead since birth.'

'Strength of will,' was the flat reply.

The two men occupied the table next to Abbie's. They'd been arguing for the last fifteen minutes, and she had been shamelessly listening. She didn't have anything to do; and, besides, she'd always been an inveterate eavesdropper. It was part of her nature. It was also part of her job.

This wasn't what you'd call a heated argument. It sounded like the kind of disagreement good friends have when one of them has done something the other considers imprudent or irresponsible or just plain dumb. In this case, the scruffier of the two apparently had made a bet that qualified—in his friend's eyes, at least—as all three.

Over the years Abbie had become adept at pretending not to be aware of or interested in what was going on around her.

As she continued to eavesdrop on the men at the next table, she reflected that they were both undeniably macho types. But then this was Oklahoma, smack in the middle of the Great American West, where men were men and their womenfolk liked them that way. Or so the men would have you believe.

These two, however, didn't quite fit the sterotype of the rugged Western male. For one thing, neither of them was wearing a cowboy hat or a shirt with a topstitched yoke and mother-of-pearl snaps down the front. For another, though they both spoke with a distinctive Oklahoma twang, they weren't bothering to conceal the fact that they were well-educated. Abbie suspected that most of the men she'd met recently would have cut out their tongues rather than admit that they'd atte.ided college.

She had arrived in this small town south-east of Tulsa eight days ago to cover a demonstration against a proposed nuclear power plant. Most of the protesters were native Americans who were violently opposed to the idea of having a nuclear facility constructed on land adjacent to their tribal cemetery. Abbie had figured she'd be able to sell the story as a human interest piece to two or three local newspapers, at best. Then, two days before the demonstration was to take place, some idiot at the Bureau of Indian Affairs had suggested that the 'remains' be relocated to 'a mutually acceptable area', and suddenly her moderately interesting little human interest story had turned into page one news.

As the only freelance journalist on the scene, she immediately received frantic phone calls from desperate editors at most of the major eastern newspapers. Few of them had considered one more anti-nuclear demonstration important enough to assign a staff reporter to cover.

Consequently, Abbie had been able to pick and choose from the offers she received. The day before the demonstration, she made a very lucrative deal with *The Washington Post*. She had filed the wrap-up story several hours ago, but, since the first available flight to New York wouldn't leave Tulsa until the next morning, she found herself with the rest of the day and what promised to be a long night to kill.

A frown marred Abbie's wide forehead as she poked at the maraschino cherry floating in her drink. The demonstration hadn't been the only reason she'd trekked all the way to the wilds of Oklahoma. She had hoped that once that story was out of the way, she might manage to track down the area's most famous native—and gather enough information to write a feature article about the reclusive engineer-inventor.

Malachi Garrett. She'd learned during the past couple of days that speaking it aloud was guaranteed to make the town's normally friendly, talkative citizens clam up and start eyeing her with suspicion and mistrust.

When she had mentioned this strange reaction to the local sheriff, he'd merely shrugged and told her that: a) folks in this neck of the woods respected a person's privacy; and b) since both Garrett's dislike of reporters and his rotten temper were well known, it was doubtful she'd find anybody brave enough or foolish enough to gossip about him. Which meant, damn it, that the story about Malachi Garrett wasn't going to be written. At least, not by her.

She was debating whether to go up to her room and console herself with a bubble bath, when something one of the men at the next table said caught her attention.

'I designed the damn engine, Deke, and I'm telling you there's no way she can win. There's just no way.'

'I designed the damn engine . . .

Abbie dismissed the sudden spurt of excitement she felt as foolish, ridiculous. Just look at him, for Pete's sake—baggy, grease-strained grey sweatshirt, faded jeans, also stained, and worn blue jogging shoes over white athletic socks. He looked as if he hadn't been anywhere near a barber for months, though at least he was clean-shaven. She continued to study him surreptitiously as she swirled the ice around in her glass.

Nice, strong jaw. Impressive shoulders. Shiny, healthy-looking hair, even if it was too long for her taste. It was a dark, glossy brown, luxuriantly thick and straight. He wore it brushed back from his face, but a deep wave dipped rebelliously over each temple. Abbie was admiring those waves from beneath lowered lashes when his companion responded to what he'd said.

'You're forgetting one minor detail, aren't you. Mal?' he asked drily. 'This new design of yours may be a masterpiece of engineering, but an engine ain't worth spit without an experienced driver. Somebody's gotta *drive* the danged car, and we both know that somebody isn't gonna be you. You're the worst driver this side of the Mississippi.'

The other man scowled darkly, but he didn't dispute the remark about his driving. 'I'll find a driver,' he muttered. 'It doesn't have to be somebody local,' he argued stubbornly. 'That wasn't part of the bet. I thought I'd make a few calls, see if I can get hold of Southfield, or maybe Ferris.'

Deke shook his head. His expression looked almost pitying. 'Mal, it's the middle of May. They're both racing at Indy this year, aren't they? They'll be tied up with time trials all month.'

'Oh, hell, I forgot about that.'

Abbie found it hard to believe that a mechanic from Oklahoma would know Dave Southfield and Tony Ferris

—two of the most famous formula one race drivers in the world—well enough to consider asking either of them to drive a car for him . . . presumably so that he could win this bet he'd made. When the waiter came by, she asked him if he knew the men at the other table.

The young man's head bobbed in affirmation. 'Yeah, the one who looks like he just crawled out of a diesel engine is Malachi Garrett. The other one's Mr Craddock . . . Deke Craddock. Have they been hassling you? Don't be afraid to say yes, if they have. Everybody knows Mal Garrett's a . . . well, a woman-hater, I guess is what you'd call him.'

Abbie suspected that the waiter had no idea what she did for a living. If he'd known she was a writer hustling for a story, no doubt he'd have clammed up like everybody else the second she mentioned Garrett's name. She proceeded with caution, not wanting to tip her hand just yet.

'I've known a few men like that,' she murmured. 'Usually their attitude is the result of a bitter divorce.'

The young man nodded sagely. 'I know exactly what you mean. But that's not what turned Mal Garrett against women. He's never been married that I know of.'

Abbie lifted her glass and took a sip of ginger ale. 'Mmm, must have been an unhappy love affair, then.'

'That's what folks say. The story is that she dumped him for some big wheeler-dealer from back east—just took off one day, didn't even leave a note. The next thing anybody heard of her, her new sugar-daddy had set her up with her own engineering firm. She took everything Mal had taught her and used it to start stealing his clients.'

'You don't say?' Abbie murmured. She'd already formed a mental profile of the woman: above average intelligence, shrewd, cunning, ambitious; probably beautiful, and not the least bit hesitant to use her looks as well as her brains to get what she wanted. 'I imagine her desertion hit Mr Garrett pretty hard.'

The waiter stole a furtive glance at the next table before answering. 'You could say that,' he muttered under his breath. 'He went on a three-day binge, did a couple thousand dollars' worth of damage to Ramey's—that's the bar up the street. Sheriff Collier finally had to lock him up, before he did himself or somebody else a real injury. It took the sheriff and two deputies to get him from Ramey's over to the jail.'

'But the jail's only a block from the bar, isn't it?' Abbie asked in confusion.

The young man grinned. 'Yeah, but when Mal makes up his mind to raise hell, there's no holdin' him back. Most folks just lay low till he runs out of steam.'

Abbie was eager to wring more information out of him—subtly, of course—but just then Mr Garrett raised his voice to ask for another beer. He sounded impatient. Flushing guiltily, the waiter hurried off towards the bar.

Abbie frowned into her ginger ale. So the famous Malachi Garrett had been jilted by an ambitious lover, and as a result had become a misogynist. She had already been told, more than once, that he held all media representatives in contempt; she didn't care to speculate about what his opinion of a female freelance journalist would be. Her hopes of persuading him to grant her an interview were diminishing rapidly.

When the waiter brought Mal his beer, he conspicuously avoided making eye-contact with Abbie. Evidently he'd realised that it wasn't such a good idea to gossip about the town's number one hell-raiser when the hell-raiser himself was sitting within earshot.

'How about Fred Bender's boy?' his friend Deke

suggested helpfully. 'He's always entering demolition derbies. Usually wins a trophy, too.'

If possible, Garrett's scowl intensified. 'The idea's to get both the car and me to Washington in one piece, Deke.'

Abbie sat up straighter, her eyes widening in reaction. Both the car and *him?*

'I guess you've got a point,' Deke conceded with a grin.

'I've invested two years and close to half a million dollars in this engine. Joey Bender isn't getting within a mile of it. Hell, he'd probably have three head-on collisions before he cleared the city limit sign.'

After that last disparaging remark, both men fell silent. Abbie presumed they were trying to come up with the name of another potential driver. A plan began to take shape in her mind. She had no idea whether the Washington Malachi Garrett had referred to was Washington state or Washington, DC; but either way he was talking about a trip that would take several days to make. Several days when he and the person he selected to be his driver would be alone in the car, with only each other for company. Not giving herself time to second-guess the decision, she got up and walked over to his table.

'Excuse me?'

Mal glanced up with an impatient frown. His impatience changed to wariness approximately one second after he registered the young woman standing beside him. She wasn't from around here, that much was obvious at a glance. Her fashionably oversized white blouse looked like real silk, and he'd be willing to bet that the name on the seat of her tight blue denim jeans wasn't Levi Strauss.

Her jewellery was another tip-off that she wasn't from

this neck of the woods. A rope of pale grey pearls ended at the exact spot where her cleavage began, and a tiny five-pointed gold star adorned each earlobe. Classy, he thought with grudging approval. She was standing close enough for him to smell her expensive perfume, and on closer inspection he noticed that she was wearing three or four shades of purple eye-shadow. He doubted any of the local women owned even one shade of purple; and, if they did, they wouldn't be caught dead wearing it in public before sundown. Most of them wouldn't think of going out in public without a bra, either, he reflected as his gaze skimmed the front of her blouse and he detected the faint shadows of her nipples. One side of his mouth lifted in an appreciative smile.

Abbie endured his blatantly sexual appraisal in grim silence. It wasn't the first time a man had looked her over as if she were a brood mare being offered to the highest bidder. She'd received quite a few of those looks during the past week, though none of them had got to her quite as much as Malachi Garrett's did.

It was hard to think of him as a woman-hater, when those heavy-lidded brown eyes were subjecting her to a lazily sensual scrutiny that made her wonder if he might possess X-ray vision. Telling herself that tolerating an occassional leer was a small price to pay for an exclusive interview, she resisted the urge to cross her arms over her chest and glare at him.

Mal was aware that she didn't like the way he was looking at her. Her back was as stiff as a poker and, though her arms hung loose at her sides, her fingers were trying to curl into fists. Typical, he thought scornfully. She was probably the kind of woman who deliberately wore clothes that showed off her body, and then pretended to be offended when a man noticed what she was advertising.

In the past couple of days several people had made it their business to tell him about the lady reporter who'd been sniffing around town and asking questions about him. He wondered if the slender young woman with the purple eye-shadow and impressive chest measurement might be her. The reporter was said to be a real looker, and she certainly fitted the description.

He didn't think much of her hairstyle, though it was probably the latest fashion in New York, or wherever she came from. Her hair was a glorious colour— somewhere between gold and copper—but she'd let somebody chop it off just below her ears. Hair that thick and curly should be worn long, so that it tumbled loose over her shoulders. When he realised that he was fantasising about weaving his fingers through her non-existent shoulder-length curls, his heavy brows jerked together in an irritated frown.

'Did you want something?' He practically snarled the question, half expecting her reply to be a request for an interview. If that was what she was after, he had an answer ready that would probably weld those tiny gold stars to her earlobes.

His curt tone didn't faze Abbie. Fortunately, when patience and tact were called for, she could exercise a great deal of both. She ignored the brusque impatience in his voice and answered his question with a smile.

'I couldn't help overhearing part of your conversation.' His frown deepened. She hurried on before he could start lambasting her for eavesdropping. 'You seem to need a driver. I'd like to apply for the job.'

She could see that she'd taken him by surprise. For a second or two he just stared at her blankly. Then his mouth started to curve in amusement. Sensing that he was about to laugh in her face, Abbie rushed into speech again.

'I'm a good driver. My father was an Army man, and I was driving jeeps before I was thirteen. By the time I got my first driver's licence, I could handle every vehicle on the base—including a Sherman tank. If it's got a gearbox and something to steer with, I can drive it.' Remembering his remarks about Joey Bender, she impulsively added, 'And I've never had an accident or even a parking ticket.'

Like all good journalists, Abbie knew when to speak her piece and when to shut up. She also knew that there were occasions—especially when she was dealing with a reluctant or hostile subject—when a well-timed silence was the most effective strategy she could employ. An abrupt, expectant silence made some people so uncomfortable that they were compelled to start talking just to end it. And the things they blurted out without thinking often were much more interesting than the information her persistent, methodical questioning had elicited.

When she saw Mal Garrett's eyes narrow and the way his lips thinned in impatience, she knew that the strategy wasn't going to work with him. He wasn't even going to consider letting her drive his car. He was going to turn her down flat, she just knew he was—and for no other reason than because she was a woman. She grappled with frustration, indignation and an unwelcome twinge of disappointment as her glittering blue-green eyes held his enigmatic brown ones.

'Looks like this is your lucky day, Mal.' His friend Deke slipped Abbie an encouraging wink as he drawled the observation.

Mal favoured him with a mildly annoyed look before swinging his gaze back to Abbie. 'You don't even know where I need the car driven,' he said flatly.

She covered her slight hesitation with a shrug. 'I heard

you mention Washington. I assumed you meant Washington DC. I have a job waiting there, provided I can get there by next Monday.'

Mal leaned back in his chair and folded his arms across his chest. He didn't say anything right away, just subjected her to a concentrated, narrow-eyed stare. Abbie tried to convince herself that his expression wasn't really as suspicious as she thought it was. It was just her guilty conscience making her over-react. He couldn't possibly know who she was or what she was up to.

'This job that's supposed to be waiting for you,' Mal finally said in a deceptively soft murmur, 'it wouldn't happen to be with a newspaper, would it?'

Abbie somehow managed to limit her reaction to a startled blink. 'A newspaper?' Miraculously, her voice conveyed only mild surprise. 'Why . . . no.' Think of something, for pity's sake! 'It's in a doctor's office. I'm a medical secretary.'

She forced herself not to fidget while she endured another long, assessing stare from those narrowed eyes. Did he believe her? Eventually he released a heavy sigh and leaned forward, resting his arms on the table.

'I don't think . . .' he began quietly.

Abbie heard the flat rejection in his voice. Evidently so did his friend. Deke interrupted before Mal could finish.

'Why don't we take her out to the farm and let her drive the car around the track a few times?' he suggested. 'Find out if she's as good as she claims to be.'

'And what if she's not?' Mel countered.

Deke hitched his shoulders in a negligent shrug. 'There's nothin' out there for her to run into. The worst she could do would be to get stuck in the mud. And if she did, we could use the tractor to pull her out.'

Mal still looked reluctant. 'Dammit, Deke, she's a woman!'

Abbie gritted her teeth to keep from blurting out something she was sure she would immediately regret, and reminded herself how badly she wanted an interview with this man.

'Noticed that, did you?' Deke drawled in amusement. Before Mal could respond, he added earnestly, 'Come on, give her a chance. What have you got to lose? You need a driver and she needs a ride east. Sounds a perfect arrangement to me.'

Mal's dour expression made it clear that he didn't agree, but apparently he wasn't able to come up with a good reason to veto Deke's suggestion.

'Oh, hell,' he muttered after a moment. 'All right, you win.'

The rush of exhilaration Abbie felt almost made her forget her resentment at being talked about as if she weren't there. She was going to be able to write her Malachi Garrett story, after all!

Deke was grinning as he rose from his chair and held out a long, bony hand. Abbie clasped it firmly, resisting the urge to throw her arms around him in gratitude.

'The name's Deke Craddock,' he said as he worked her arm like a pump handle. 'And this mean-tempered so-and-so is known as Mal Garrett, among other things. Don't pay him any mind—his bark's worse than his bite.'

'No, it isn't,' Mal denied as he pushed his chair away from the table and slowly unfolded his rangy frame from it.

For some reason, Abbie had expected him to be bigger. He was roughly the same height as Deke and probably weighed fifteen or twenty pounds less—there was no sign of a beer belly under Malachi Garrett's sweatshirt. His body was lean and hard, all muscles and sinew.

'What's your name?' he asked tersely. Abbie noticed with a feeling of relief that he didn't offer his hand. If his handshake was as vigorous as Deke's, he'd probably dislocate her shoulder. She responded to the brusque impatience in his voice by automatically providing her full name.

'Abigail Prudence Kincaid.'

Unexpectedly Mal's lips twitched in amused surprise. 'Abigail Prudence?'

Abbie was uncomfortably aware that she was blushing. 'That's right,' she muttered self-consciously. 'But everybody calls me Abbie.'

There was a mocking gleam in his eyes as he gestured towered the door to the lobby. 'Well, Abigail Prudence . . .' He deliberately used both names, his deep, lazy drawl daring her to object. 'Let's go find out if you're as good a driver as you say you are.'

Abbie didn't responded to the challenge. At least, not out loud. By the time she'd collected her bag from the other table, both he and Deke Craddock were half-way to the door. She hurried after them.

Arrogant swine, she thought as she glared at Malachi Garrett's broad back. So he wanted a demonstration of her driving skill, did he? Her mouth curved in a slightly malicious smile. Well, she could do her best not to disappoint him.

CHAPTER TWO

ABBIE'S muscles ached from the strain of trying to hold herself erect on the hard bench seat of Deke's pick-up truck. For the past half-hour she'd been sandwiched between Deke on the left and Malachi Garrett on the right—neither of whom had offered to initiate a conversation after they left the hotel—while the vehicle barrelled down one rutted gravel road after another. When the truck hit another pot-hole and she was thrown against Garrett's shoulder for perhaps the twentieth time, she gritted her teeth and asked a bit desperately, 'How much farther is it?'

Deke took his attention from the road long enough to give her a sympathetic smile. 'Sorry it's been such a rough ride, but Mal insists on doing all his R and D work out at the farm.'

' "R and D Work"?' Abbie repeated, deliberately sounding confused.

'Research and development,' Mal provided.

His bored, slightly patronising tone set her teeth on edge. She affected a puzzled frown as she faced him. 'Research? What kind of research? I figured you were just a mechanic who'd built a car out of spare parts or something.'

The remark made him stiffen in offence. Deke, on the other hand, hooted with laughter.

'A mechanic! Wait till the boys in town hear that!'

Mal ignored his friend's outburst. 'For your information, Abigail Prudence Kincaid,' he replied irritably, 'I possess engineering degrees from three of the top universities in the country, including a doctorate from MIT.'

Abbie feigned sceptical amusement. 'No kidding?' Her tone implied that she suspected he was pulling her leg.

'No kidding,' he confirmed tersely.

'You're putting me on . . . aren't you?' He gave her a withering look, but didn't deign to reply. 'Well, if you're telling the truth, how come you go around looking like that?' she challenged. 'You look like a bum.'

'She's got you there, Mal,' Deke said soberly. Once again he was ignored.

Abbie watched Mal Garrett closely, alert to every nuance of expression on his rugged face. She sensed that his pride was ruffled, but that he was stubbornly resisting the urge to defend or explain his grubby appearance. There was arrogant disdain in the strong line of his jaw, and also a hint of resentment; yet she thought she saw a glimmer of surprise beneath his lowered lashes. She concluded that he probably wasn't used to such a blunt honesty, at least not from a woman. She had begun to think he wasn't going to respond to her unflattering remarks, when his mouth suddenly quirked in a wry half-smile and he drawled a laconic, 'Thanks.'

Well, at least he possessed a sense of humour. Encouraged, Abbie decided to press for more information. 'Have you been working on this car you built?'

Before Mal could answer, the truck hit another hole and Abbie pitched to the right, straight toward his lap. Without thinking, she threw both arms out to brace herself. The next thing she knew, he had her clamped firmly against his side. Her startled eyes flew to his face. His cool ones were waiting to capture and hold her gaze.

The breath she'd just inhaled inexplicably became trapped in her lungs. How was it that she hadn't noticed that deep cleft in his chin before now, or that he possessed eyelashes any woman would envy?

'OK?' he asked with a slight frown.

Or how deep and incredibly sexy his voice was, she added silently as she finally exhaled.

'Yes. Fine.' She was aware that she sounded a little short of breath, and it irritated her. What was wrong with her, for heaven's sake? So, he was an attractive man. She'd known attractive men before; dozens of them, in fact.

She started to pull herself upright and belatedly realised that one of her hands was resting on the front of his sweatshirt and the other hand landed on his thigh. And pretty far up on his thigh, at that. She hastily withdrew them both, but when she tried to edge away from him, Mal didn't seem inclined to let her.

'You might as well stay where you are,' he told her. 'The last stretch of road is the worst.'

Abbie soon discovered that he hadn't been exaggerating. By the time Deke steered the truck off the road and on to a narrow gravel drive, her teeth felt loose. Thankfully, the drive had been kept in much better condition than the roads. As soon as they were headed down it, Mal slipped his arm from around her. Abbie wasted no time scooting back to the centre of the seat.

Evidently they had arrived at 'the farm'. Straight ahead was a white two-story house with dark green shutters. To the left of the house stood a big red barn. The doors of the barn were standing open and a wrought-iron weather-vane turned lazily on the roof. Both the house and barn looked freshly painted and were obviously well maintained. To the right was a third building, larger and newer than the barn. Probably some kind of equipment shed, Abbie thought as Deke parked his truck next to the building.

'Well, here we are,' he announced with a grin. 'Ready to take the test drive, or do you need to rest a bit first?'

'That depends,' Abbie said drily. 'Will I have to drive on the same roads you took to get us out here?'

It was Mal who answered, as he opened his door and stepped down from the cab. 'No. There's a test track out back.'

Abbie grimaced as she slid across the seat. 'Paved, I hope.'

His fleeting smile surprised her, but not as much as the casual way he reached up to grasp her waist and lift her out of the truck. He didn't step back, so that when he released her there were only a few inches of space between them.

'If I said no, would you back out?'

The soft challenge made Abbie draw herself up to her full five feet six inches. She looked straight into his eyes as she answered. 'No, I wouldn't. I told you, I have to get to Washington by next Monday.'

'Right,' he drawled. 'You have a job waiting.'

Something in his voice—scepticism? outright disbelief?—made Abbie tense with wariness. 'That's right.'

'In a doctor's office,' he murmured. Now his voice carried no inflection at all, which worried her even more.

'Yes.' Seeking to distract him, she turned toward the building. 'Is the car you built inside?'

She tried to convince herself she only imagined that he hesitated briefly before answering. 'Yes. But I didn't build the entire car, just the parts that make it go.'

He led the way through a metal door set into the side of the building. Abbie followed, with Deke right behind her. She wasn't sure wht she'd expected, but it definitely hadn't been the ultra-modern, almost sterile-looking environment they entered. Her first impression was that it reminded her of a hospital operating room. It was that clean and bright. She half expected someone in surgical greens to step forward and present them with masks and rubber gloves. She didn't see anyone dressed like a doctor on the way to surgery, but there were several people engrossed in work of some sort. They all wore immaculate white overalls and matching canvas shoes.

The door banged shut behind them. Mal stopped and turned to Abbie, one heavy brow forming an expectant arch.

'Is this where you work?' She didn't try to hide her surprise.

'This is it.' He indicated the people intent on their various task. 'These guys are all master mechanics. They work for me,' he added, just in case she'd failed to draw the obvious conclusion.

'Fascinating,' she murmured with a marked lack of sincerity. 'I'm curious—how am I supposed to drive this car of yours, when the engine seems to be in a million pieces?'

'Not to worry,' he assured her. 'I always stock at least three of every component. The ones that are being tested are spares. The car's ready . . . if you are.'

His slight pause was as much a challenge as the words that followed it. Abbie squared her slender shoulders and nodded briskly. 'I'm ready, Mr Garrett. Lead me to it.'

A few of the mechanics spared time from their work to glance at her curiously as she followed Mal and Deke through the garage. The car was parked at the rear, behind a wall of sophisticated electronic equipment. When Abbie got her first glimpse of it, she came to a surprised halt. A second later she was hurrying forward with an excited exclamation.

'A Shelby Cobra! A sixty-eight model, isn't it?' Not waiting for an answer, she started circling the car for a closer look, trailing her fingertips over the gleaming black body as if she had to touch it to assure herself that it was real.

'Yes.' Clearly Mal was surprised that she'd known what it was, much less been able to name the model year. 'Have you ever driven a Cobra?' he asked as he faced her over the roof.

Abbie shook her head with a rueful smile. 'No such luck. My older brother had one when I was a kid, but he'd traded it for a newer model by the time Dad let me start driving.'

Mel stepped closer to the car, lifting his arms to rest them on the roof. Evidently this snippet of her family history had captured his interest. 'Oh, yeah? What did he trade it for?'

'Another Mustang,' Abbie answered as she bent to peek through the driver's window. 'A seventy-two. I told him he was crazy. The Shelby was twice as good-looking.' She was grinning when she straightened. 'Twice as fast, too. It could blow the doors off everything else on the base, including the CO's Corvette.'

A spark of indulgent amusement flickered in Mal's eyes. 'You like fast cars, do you?'

Abbie sensed that he'd temporarily let himself forget that she was female, and therefore the enemy. She instinctively sought to take advantage of their tentative rapport. In order to do an in-depth story about him, she needed to find a way around his antagonism and mistrust and get to know the Mal Garrett his closest friends knew—the man of whom Deke had said. 'His bark's worse than his bite.'

'You bet I do,' she replied honestly. 'Don't you?

He shrugged. 'For me, speed isn't as important as overall engine performance. But yes, I like fast cars.'

'Otherwise he wouldn't have kept that old Cobra all these years,' Deke added. 'It was your first car, wasn't it, Mal?'

A soft, reminiscent smile made his already attractive mouth look positively sensual as he nodded. Abbie watched his long fingers caress the highly waxed surface of the car's roof, and shocked herself by wondering how they would feel moving over her body that way. What on earth was wrong with her? What had happened to her professional detachment, her objectivity?

'How old were you?' Abbie asked.

He glanced at her in surprise. She had the feeling that he'd momentarily forgotten she was there. 'Seventeen.' His tone was suddenly brusque, almost curt. 'We're wasting time.' He walked around the car to select a crash helmet from several resting on a shelf behind Abbie. 'This looks like the right size,' he said, handing it to her.

Her lips twitched in amusement as she examined the gleaming white helmet. 'Do you really think it's necessary for me to wear this?'

Mal's expression hardened noticeably. 'Let me put it this way: no helmet, no test drive. No test drive, no deal.'

It was on the tip of her tongue to ask him if she'd be required to wear the helmet all the way to Washington, but she curbed the impulse and instead settled it firmly on her head.

'Exactly what do you want me to do, once I get the car on to the track?'

Mal's faint smile was infuriatingly supercilious. 'Just try to complete two full laps without ending up axle-deep in the mud.'

It was obvious that he didn't expect her to complete even one full lap without losing control of the car.

'Fine.' She turned away slightly, pretending to adjust the helmet's chin-strap while she brought her temper under control. She glared at the shelf from which Mal had taken her helmet while she struggled to subdue her indignant outrage. Her eyes suddenly widened. An instant later they narrowed shrewdly. When she turned back to the car, she was holding a bright red helmet a couple of sizes larger than the white one she had been bullied into wearing. Mal's shaggy brows jerked down over his nose when she thrust it into his hands.

'You can't judge my driving by watching me from the garage door.' She spoke calmly, reasonably, careful to keep any hint of challenge out of her voice. 'The only way to make a fair judgement is to ride with me.'

Mal's frown became a scowl as he racked his brain for a reason to refuse to get into the car with her. Abbie quickly opened the door on the driver's side and slid behind the wheel before he could come up with one.

'Well?' She let just a trace of impatience creep into her voice as she turned to Mal in question. 'Are you coming, or not? A minute ago you complained that we were wasting time.'

She pretended not to see the dark look he shot her as he reluctantly donned the red helmet and ducked into the car. She twisted the key in the ignition before he could change his mind and climb back out. The engine instantly roared to life, and she just heard his muttered objection.

'Sorry.' Abbie flashed a smile that she hoped looked apologetic. 'I barely tapped the accelerator, honest. It must need some adjustment.'

Mal glared at her as if she'd deliberately insulted him. 'There's nothing wrong with the accelerator,' he informed her coldly. 'This happens to be a finely tuned piece of machinery, Miss Kincaid, not that I expect you to appreciate the fact.'

'You're the mechanic,' she said with studied indifference. The jibe produced exactly the result she'd expected: his features tautened, his nostrils pinching as he inhaled sharply. 'Oh, excuse me . . . the *engineer*,' she corrected in a tone that made it clear she was only humouring him. 'The point is, I only have to be able to drive the car, and I assure you, Mr Garrett, I *can* drive it.'

His lips thinned in a glacial smile. 'I'll be the judge of that. It's time to back up your talk with some action, Abigail Prudence Kincaid.' He inclined his head toward the open door at the rear of the building as he buckled himself into his seat. 'The track is straight ahead. Let's see if you can really drive, or if you're just full of hot air.'

So he wanted to back up her words with action, did he? All right, she told him silently as she willed her tensed muscles to relax. Just remember, Buster, you asked for it.

Her brows furrowed in concentration.

'The clutch feels stiff,' she murmured as the Shelby's rear bumper cleared the garage door. 'Did you just put it in?'

'Yeah, a couple of days ago.'

The disgruntled note in Mal's voice didn't escape her notice. No doubt he'd expected her to either kill the engine or make the car buck like a mechanical bull when she released the clutch. As soon as she'd steered the car on to the asphalt surface of the track, she braked it to a smooth stop.

'I'll take it easy for the first couple of laps . . . get a feel for how she handles,' she said casually.

Mal's indifferent shrug didn't fool her. 'Suit yourself,' he muttered. 'You're the driver.'

'That's right,' Abbie replied coolly. She didn't see the irritated look Mal shot her. All her attention, all her awareness, were already concentrated on the car. She was so absorbed in learning the rhythm of this particular car's idling engine that she didn't notice the speculative glint in Mal's narrowed eyes as he observed her from the other bucket seat.

When she realised for the first time how much power the engine was capable of generating, she experienced an almost intoxicating rush of exhilaration. She wasn't aware of the smile that tugged at the corners of her mouth, but Mal saw it. His gaze sharpened, but he didn't speak.

She accelerated cautiously as soon as the track straightened out again, speed-shifting into fourth gear with the confident skill of a pro. The needle of the speedometer was nudging the sixty-mile-per-hour mark when she downshifted to take the second banked curve. The car shot around it beautifully. They finished the first lap at an even seventy miles per hour.

'Did you completely redesign the engine?' Abbie yelled the question in order to be heard above the wind rushing in through the open windows.

Mal's shouted reply sounded a little testy. 'No. I kept the original, but I've made substantial modifications to it.'

They whizzed around the second curve and completed lap two. The speedometer registered eighty-two miles per hour. 'What's top end?' she asked.

'I don't know exactly.'

Abbie was incredulous. 'You redesigned the engine, and you don't know how fast the car will go?'

He shifted restlessly in the other bucket seat. 'Did you hear what Deke said back at the hotel . . . about my driving?' He waited for her nod, then confessed gruffly,

'Well, it's true. I'm a lousy driver.'

Abbie sensed that the admission had been made at considerable cost to his pride. 'Well, isn't there anyone else who could have tested it for you—maybe Deke, or one of the mechanics?'

He made a rude noise. 'No way. I've got too much time and money invested in this baby to trust it to just anybody.'

Yet he had agreed to let her test drive the car. Abbie wondered if he was aware that his attitude toward her had undergone a subtle change. It still couldn't be called cordial, by any means, but at least his voice held grudging respect now.

If she could get him to think of her as a qualified driver first and a woman second, maybe he would let down his guard, start to relax with her. Friendly would be even better, but she would happily settle for comfortably relaxed. Otherwise, she could kiss her dream of an exclusive Malachi Garrett story goodbye.

From now on, she decided impulsively, she would make herself as sexless as possible. She was confident that her strategy would work; before long Mr Malachi Garrett would be thinking of her as just one of the guys.

Five minutes later Abbie steered the car off the track and back into the garage. Neither she nor Mal had uttered a word after his response. She had no idea what he was thinking, and she was reluctant to look at him, even after she'd shut off the engine.

It had belatedly occurred to her that in attempting to prove herself, she might have gone a little too far. She'd had time for one quick glance at the speedometer as they entered the straightway that last time around the track, and what she'd seen had made her decide to quit while she was ahead—the needle had been hovering directly over the one hundred and twenty mile per hour mark.

She'd been startled, and, if she was honest, a little unnerved. The Shelby handled so beautifully and gave such a smooth ride that it was hard to believe they were travelling at that speed, even after she'd seen the evidence with her own eyes.

She still didn't speak as she removed the white helmet and ran nervous fingers through her hair. When she she heard his door open, her head snapped around, her eyes wide and questioning. He was climbing out of the car. Abbie hurried to follow suit.

'Holy catfish!' The exclamation came from Deke, as he hurried into the garage to join them. 'That is one hot car, Mal. And one hot driver!' he added with a huge grin. Without warning, he swooped down on Abbie, lifting her off the floor for an exuberant bear hug. When he set her back on her feet, she stared at him dazedly.

'Thank you.'

She didn't think Deke heard her. His attention had shifted back to Mal. 'Well?' he said expectantly. 'How about it? You have to admit she did everything you asked of her.'

'And then some,' Mal agreed as he removed the red helmet and placed it on the shelf.

Abbie started to speak up, then changed her mind. She waited silently while he raked both hands through his hair and heaved a sigh that could have conveyed either resignation or disgust. He suddenly turned, his narrowed eyes capturing and holding her anxious gaze.

'I'm curious,' he murmured. 'How did a medical secretary from Washington, DC, end up stranded in a one-horse town in the middle of Oklahoma?'

Abbie frantically cast about for a plausible story, one he would be likely to accept without too many questions.

'Well, I was with my boyfriend,' she improved hastily. Carrying her helmet back to the shelf from which he'd taken it gave her an excuse to turn away from his probing gaze.

'Your boyfriend,' Mal repeated. He leaned back against the Shelby, arms folded over his chest. His narrowed eyes continued to scrutinise her.

'That's right. We came out west to visit his sister.' She placed her helmet next to his, giving herself a few more seconds to think before turning back to face him.

'Frankly, the trip was a bummer. The night we got there, Larry's sister accused her husband of having an affair with her best friend. After that, they were constantly at each other's throats. It was a pretty uncomfortable situation, so we decided to cut the visit short and headed home a few days early. I'd have been half-way to Washington by now, but we had a big fight just this side of Tulsa. Larry waited until I was asleep, then cut out—left me stranded in some fleabag motel. I didn't even know he was gone till the next morning.'

Mal's brows snapped together in surprise . 'He just took off and left you?'

'High and dry,' Abbie confirmed with a straight face.

'That must have been some fight.'

She shrugged.

Mal's expression was sceptical, to say the least, but he refrained from voicing any doubts he may have had about her scruples, or lack of them. 'So how did you come to be at the hotel in town?'

'I managed to get this far by hitch-hiking, but I don't like taking rides from strangers, and I didn't see how I could possibly get all the way to Washington by next Monday. To make matters worse, Larry only left me enough to pay for a hotel room for a couple of nights. I was feeling pretty low, I don't mind telling you. And then I happened to overhear you and Deke talking about how you needed a driver to get you and your car to

Washington, and . . . well, it seemed like fate or something.'

Mal's mouth quirked in a reluctant half-smile. Their gazes locked for just a moment, and Abbie thought he was about to speak. But then he suddenly pushed away from the car and walked around it, heading for the front of the building. He tossed a careless instruction over his shoulder, almost as an afterthought.

'Take her back to the hotel, Deke.'

CHAPTER THREE

FOR a second or two Abbie was too stunned to react. Then she swore under her breath and went after him.

'Hey, wait a minute!'

Mal didn't even slow down. She caught up with him half-way through the garage, then had to take two steps to his one to keep up as he made for the door by which they'd originally entered the building.

'Why does he have to take me back to the hotel?' she demanded as she trotted along at his side. 'Just what was wrong with my driving?'

Mal stopped abruptly when he reached the door. 'Not a thing. You've got the job, Miss Kincaid.'

Abbie just stared at him for a moment, afraid to trust her hearing. 'You mean . . . you're going to let me drive you to Washington?'

He gave her an impatient, slightly exasperated look. 'Wasn't that what you wanted?'

She could hardly believe her luck. 'Yes!' she blurted before he could change his mind. 'But if you've decided to let me drive, why did you just tell Deke——'

'You'll need to collect your things. We leave at noon tomorrow, which doesn't give you much time to become familiar with the car. You can stay out here tonight and get in some more practice time after supper.'

Abbie had barely registered the fact that he intended for her to spend the night at the farm when he opened the door and stepped outside.

'Wait!' She rushed after him, impulsively grabbing his

arm to stop him. Now that she knew her exculsive Malachi Garrett story would become a reality, there were one or two last-minute things she needed to take care of— such as calling the editor at the *Post* who'd bought her anti-nuclear piece to ask if he would also be interested in buying this one. She couldn't make that call from Malachi Garrett's house; not unless she wanted to risk blowing both her cover and the story.

Mal's gazed dropped to the slender fingers clutching his arm. One shaggy brow arched in surprise. Abbie snatched her hand away at once, loath to have him think she was coming on to him.

'You—er—want to me spend the night here?' She barely stopped herself from adding, 'With you?' Judging by his reaction, she might as well have gone ahead and said it.

'No need to get yourself in a dither, Abigail Prudence.' He subjected her to a slow head-to-toe appraisal, allowing his gaze to linger for several seconds on the front of her blouse. 'Your virtue is safe, believe me.'

Abbie almost winced at the mocking emphasis he gave the word 'virtue'. He couldn't have made it any more clear that he considered hers to be in extremely short supply.

'Oh, I wasn't worried about that,' she assured him. 'Actually, I was thinking of you. Aren't you concerned about what people might think—your friends, I mean, and the people in town? Or do you make a habit of picking up strange women in bars and then moving them into your house?'

She regretted the taunt the second it left her mouth. She saw irritation flicker briefly in his eyes, and the way his sensual mouth thinned slightly, and braced herself for the worst.

'I can see this is going to be a long trip,' he muttered.

Abbie hastily attempted to placate him. 'Listen, I didn't mean to be . . . well, insulting.'

His eyebrows rose a sceptical centimetre but, other than that, he didn't comment. She offered him a tentative, ingratiating smile.

'I don't always think before I speak.'

'Do tell.' His tone was as dry as dust.

Abbie abandoned hope of convincing him to let her stay at the hotel that night. At this point, she would consider herself lucky if he didn't call off their arrangement and send her packing. She impulsively decided that a touch of humility was called for.

'I really am sorry if I offended you. I don't know what comes over me sometimes. You'd think I didn't have a brain in my head, the way I just blurt out any old——'

'Save it, Abigail. It's a little late to start playing a dizzy blonde. You don't have to worry that I'll back out of our deal. I won't pretend I'm overjoyed to have you as my chauffeur. We both know I'm not. But you're the best driver I'm likely to find before noon tomorrow, so I guess I'm stuck with you.'

'And vice versa.' The dry rejoinder was out before Abbie could stop it. Thankfully, Mal didn't bother to acknowledge it.

'And the answer to your question is no,' he continued as if she hadn't spoken. 'I don't make a habit of picking up strange women in bars, much less inviting them to move into my house.' He sounded as if, given the choice, he would prefer to share his home with a colony of scorpions.

'I didn't really think so,' Abbie confessed. 'I was just . . .'

'Needling me,' Mal finished for her. 'As you've been doing for the last couple of hours.'

She felt her face heat with a guilty flush. 'Well . . .

yes. For some reason you seem to bring out the shrew in me.'

He smiled, but it was a thin, wintry sort of smile; the kind that conveys dwindling patience, rather than amusement.

'Yeah, I noticed that,' he murmured. He paused to rake a lean brown hand through his hair. For the first time, Abbie noticed the dark circles under his eyes. There was also a definite droop to his broad shoulders as he leaned back against the garage wall. The man was exhausted, she realized with a small jolt of surprise—wiped out, dead on his feet.

'This trip is very important to me, for several reasons,' he said quietly. Now that she listened for it, she heard the exhaustion in his voice, too. 'I'm going to have enough on my mind, without having to contend with a wise-ass feminist who feels obliged to get in at least one or two digs per mile.'

Abbie decided to let the 'wide-ass' pass—for the time being, anyway. 'What makes you think I'm a feminist?' she asked in as mild a tone as she could manage.

Another thin smile slashed his mouth. 'What made you take one look at me and decide I was a male chauvinist pig?' he countered.

Abbie decided that at least they were in agreement about one thing: it *was* going to be a long trip. 'Instinct,' she answered succinctly.

Mal's head dipped in a brusque nod. 'Exactly. So we both know where we stand—neither of us is thrilled with our little arrangement. Unfortunately, like it or not, we're going to be spending virtually every minute together for the next few days.'

'In other words,' Abbie surmised drily, 'it would be in both our interests to agree to a temporary truce in the battle between the sexes.'

'I'd say it should be our number one priority,' he drawled. 'Tell you what—I'll try not to come on like such a chauvinist swine, if you'll make an effort not to be such a . . . pain in the neck.'

He'd almost said 'bitch'. Abbie was sure of it. She gave him half a point for self-restraint. Pasting on a smile that felt stiff, she offered her hand.

'You've got a deal, Mr Garrett.'

As his hard, warm fingers closed around hers, she thought wryly that, while she had every intention of keeping her part of the bargain—she had a powerful incentive, after all—it was highly doubtful that he would be able to do the same. She told herself that it didn't matter. She was determined to get to know the real Malachi Garrett, the man behind the legend. If that man turned out to be an incorrigible sexist, which she suspected would be the case, that was precisely how her story would portray him.

Deke drove her back to town in his pick-up truck. When they arrived at the hotel, Abbie suggested that he relax in the bar with a cold beer while she packed and checked out. He agreed willingly.

Fortunately, she'd already done most of her packing. She dug the notebook containing the *Post's* telephone number out of her purse and placed it beside the phone, then quickly punched out the phone number. A glance at her watch caused two deep creases to appear between her brows. Deke had already had time to finish one beer and start on a second.

'Will somebody answer the stupid phone?' she muttered irritably. There was one more ring, and then a nasal female voice informed her that she'd reached the newspaper's editorial offices.

'Roger Zirkelbach, please.' Abbie used a brisk,

businesslike tone.

'One moment, please, I'll see if he's still in.'

Roger picked up his extension in the middle of the second ring. Abbie didn't waste time on pleasantries.

'It's Abbie Kincaid, Roger. Would you be interested in an exclusive piece about Malachi Garrett?'

There was utter silence at the other end of the line for several seconds. Abbie began to think she'd been cut off.

'Hell, yes, I'd be interested! But how on earth did you get to him? I thought he was supposed to be some kind of misanthrope.'

Abbie glanced at her watch again. 'It's a little complicated, and I don't have time to explain all the hows and whys. I can tell you that the story involves a cross-country race between two cars—one of which is a sixty-eight Shelby Cobra equipped with some kind of experimental engine Garrett designed.'

Roger expelled a low whistle. 'And you'll have access to all the details?' To say that he sounded excited would have been an understatement.

'Better than that,' Abbie replied. 'I'll be driving Garrett's car. Garrett will be in it, by the way. I don't know who else is involved—at least, not yet—but I think there'll only be Garrett's car and one other. I imagine the reason you haven't heard about it is because, as far as I can tell, the race is to settle a bet between Garrett and the person who designed the other car . . . or maybe just the other car's engine. That's something else I don't know yet. And don't ask me what the bet's about, or the terms, because I don't know that, either. I do know that our destination is Washington DC. I could probably deliver the story to you a few hours after we arrive.'

'I see,' Roger said. 'And did you also tell him that as well as being a driver, you're a first-rate freelance journalist?'

Abbie's mouth twisted in a rueful grimace. He was fretting about professional ethics.

'No,' she admitted reluctantly. 'I said I was a medical secretary. I had to lie,' she added quickly, before Roger could start giving her a lecture. 'He despises reporters almost as much as he despises women, and he'd never have agreed——'

Roger hastily cut her off. 'Hold it! I don't think you'd better tell me any more.' He hesitated a moment, then murmured drily, 'It sounds as if you're going to end up with one hell of a story, kid. I'll have a staff photographer waiting when you arrive. All you have to do is let me know the approximate time you'll get here and which route into the city you'll be using.'

A frown settled on Abbie's forehead. 'That might be a little difficult. Contacting you, I mean, without Garrett's knowing.' She considered the problem for a moment. 'I guess I could tell him I need to call my landlord, or the doctor I'm supposed to start working for next week.'

'Either story sounds good to me,' Roger said with an enthusiasm she didn't share. 'Now that I think of it, it would be a good idea for you to contact me at regular intervals during the trip, too—keep me informed about how the race is going.'

Abbie's spine stiffened in alarm. 'I can't agree to that,' she protested. 'I might be able to sneak in one or two phone calls, but Garrett would be sure to suspect something if I called Washington every time we stopped for fuel.'

'You're probably right,' Roger conceded reluctantly. 'But I'd still like to be brought up to date as often as possible. Use your own judgement. Call me whenever you think it's safe. I'd better give you my home number, in case you have to call at night.'

Abbie jotted down his home telephone number in her

notebook, beside the one for the *Post*. Then she told Roger that she really *had* to go, and rang off before any more questions or unreasonable requests could occur to him.

Fortunately the clerk at the front desk wasn't busy, so it only took a couple of minutes to check out. Abbie then picked up her suitcase and hurried for the hotel bar. She paused in the doorway to scan the room for Deke.

When she spotted him, she almost dropped the suitcase. Deke was seated at a table approximately halfway across the room, engrossed in conversation with another man. From their relaxed posture and the way they both laughed at something Deke had just said, it was obvious that they knew each other well.

The man sitting with Deke was Sheriff Collier.

CHAPTER FOUR

DAMN!

For several interminable seconds Abbie stood frozen in indecision. Squaring her shoulders, she walked directly to the table. Both men looked up when she stopped and deposited her suitcase on the floor. Deke jumped to his feet with a welcoming smile. The sheriff also stood, but he wasn't smiling. Abbie's pulse skittered nervously.

'Sorry I took so long,' she said before either man could speak. 'Sheriff Collier, what a pleasant surprise! I didn't expect to see you again.'

Whatever the sheriff was thinking, he didn't seem eager to blurt out any damning revelations about her. His green eyes met Abbie's levelly as he touched the brim of his hat in greeting.

'Evenin', Miss Kincaid. Deke tells me you're movin' out to the Garrett place.'

Abbie wavered between panic and cautious optimism. She willed herself to hold the sheriff's steady gaze as she replied. 'Yes, but only for tonight. Mr Garrett was kind enough to invite me.'

Deke's snort of disbelief gave her an excuse to shift her attention to him. 'Knowin' Mal, I suspect it was more like an order than an invitation,' he said drily. He slipped Sheriff Collier a sly wink as he added, 'But I've got a feelin' that ol' Mal may be about to meet his Waterloo.'

Abbie glanced at the sheriff to see how he'd reacted to

that last cryptic remark and caught him squelching a smile. Her tensed muscles went slack in relief. Evidently he found the situation amusing, and thankfully he didn't seem inclined to blow her cover.

Deke suddenly bent over to collect her suitcase. 'Guess we'd better be goin', Rafe,' he said to the sheriff. But when she and Deke headed for the entrance to the bar, the sheriff tagged along.

'I wish you luck on your trip, Miss Kincaid. I suspect you're going to need it.'

Before she could think of a reply that wouldn't rouse Deke's suspicion or pique his curiosity, Sheriff Collier's long legs were carrying him across the pavement to where his brown and tan patrol car was parked.

When they arrived at the farmhouse, Mal was nowhere in sight. Deke led Abbie to a bedroom on the second floor, depositing her suitcase at the foot of an old-fashioned four-poster bed. He pointed out the adjoining bathroom, then said he thought he'd go down to the garage and see if he could lend a hand with any of the last-minute details.

'If there's anything else you need, just poke around 'til you find it,' he told her with a grin. 'Mal won't mind.'

Abbie seriously doubted that, but she merely smiled and thanked Deke for playing chauffeur, assuring him that she had everything she needed. She waited until she heard the front door close behind him, then lifted her suitcase on to the bed and opened it to take out a fresh stenographer's pad. The bedroom was located at the top of the stairs, so she left the door ajar while she jotted down a few notes. If Deke or Malachi Garrett returned to the house, she would hear the front door close and have time to stash the notebook back in her suitcase.

Abbie was a compulsive meticulous note-taker. She

never completely trusted her memory of people, places or events. As a result, usually she had filled a couple of steno pads with line after line of neat script by the time she was ready to begin the actual writing process. Often her notes took the form of a personal journal, because she had discovered that her own impressions and observations were at least as important as the factual details when she began to put a story together.

When she finished recording everything that had happened that afternoon and evening, she skipped a couple of lines and printed the initials MG. Then she paused, absently tapping her pen against the notebook.

This was the point at which she usually made a list of one- or two-word descriptive tags—impressions she had formed of her subject. Abbie was surprised to discover that pinning labels on Malachi Garrett was no easy task.

The pen in her hand stopped tapping long enough for her to write the word 'paradox'.

'What else?' she murmured aloud. 'Come on, Abigail, think! What else about the man makes him special enough to write about?'

She wasn't pleased with the first answer that occurred to her: his looks.

'All right, yes,' she muttered impatiently. 'It's true, he is a good-looking man.' An incredibly sexy, good-looking man, a tiny voice inside her added. But what was there about this one that made him different . . . unique?

Well, for one thing, he didn't seem to take the slightest interest in his personal appearance.

'Eccentric' joined 'paradox' under his initials.

Abbie frowned down at the notebook in disgust.

Purely on impulse, she added three more tags, all on the same line. The list beneath Malachi Garrett's initials now read,

    paradox
    eccentric
    handsome, sexy, MCP

Irritated at her own lack of professionalism, she started to scratch out those last three entries. The tip of her ballpoint was half-way through 'handsome' when the front door suddenly slammed shut. Abbie jumped guiltily. A second later she heard someone ascending the stairs.

She barely had time to stuff the notebook and pen under a pair of jeans before the handsome, sexy male chauvinist pig himself appeared in the bedroom doorway, looking even grubbier—and, she had to admit, sexier—than she remembered. He leaned a shoulder against the doorjamb and gave her a long, level look. Abbie told herself it was foolish to imagine that those penetrating brown eyes could see right through the façade she'd created and into the secret corners of her mind.

'Is something wrong?' she asked when the silence and the intent way he was staring at her began to make her uncomfortable. 'Are you having some kind of trouble with the car?'

Mal shook his head slowly. His gaze didn't waver from her face. 'Nothing's wrong. I'm just a little surprised.'

Abbie frowned in confusion. 'Surprised?'

'That you came back with Deke.'

She stared at him blankly for a moment. 'You told me to,' she pointed out. There was a hint of exasperation in her voice, so that the statement sounded almost like an accusation. 'In fact, I'd go so far as to say you insisted.'

She could have sworn his lips twitched in the beginning of a smile. A second later she decided she'd only imagined it as she watched him straighten from the door. He stretched both arms over his head, then used his fingers to comb his hair back from his face. The hem of his sweatshirt rose a couple of inches, allowing Abbie a tantalising glimpse of taut brown flesh. The muscles in her lower abdomen contracted in reaction.

'I guess I did, at that,' he drawled. 'I threw some meat and vegetables into a pot this morning. Hopefully they've turned into some kind of a stew by now. Give me a few minutes to clean up, and we'll have supper.'

Not giving her a chance to respond, he abruptly turned and disappeared down the hall. Abbie sat staring at the empty doorway for several minutes, attempting without much success to make some sense of their brief conversation.

If Garrett had found out who she was and what she was up to, Abbie had no doubt whatsoever that she'd be on her way back to the hotel right now. Assuming she was still alive and fit to travel, of course.

Telling herself she was being paranoid, she collected the bag that held her toiletries and took it into the bathroom. What she yearned for was a long, relaxing soak in the tub, but that would have to wait. She suspected that, when Malachi Garrett said he'd only be a few minutes, that was precisely what he meant. She also suspected that he would possess little or no tolerance for any woman who kept him waiting while she primped and preened.

When every trace of make-up had been removed

and she'd brushed her hair until it crackled with static electricity, Abbie slipped the blouse back on, then took a moment to give her reflection a critical once-over. Her shoulders slumped in dismay. She looked about sixteen years old. Eighteen, tops. Thinking that a little more cleavage might add a couple of years to her appearance, she opened the top two buttons of her blouse, then quickly reconsidered and poked them back through the buttonholes when she caught a provocative glimpse of peach lace.

She glared at her reflection.

'Ready to eat?'

Abbie almost choked on a startled gasp, but the next instant she whirled around, an accusing frown drawing her delicate brows together over her nose.

'Do you always sneak up behind people like that?'

The question started out sharp with annoyance, but by the time she got to the last two words her voice had faded amost to a whisper. She struggled to collect her scattered wits and regain her composure, which had fled the instant her gaze encountered the man lounging negligently in the doorway.

Fresh from the shower, his damp hair for the moment obediently hugging his perfectly shaped skull, the hard-boned beauty of Malachi Garrett's face took her breath away. She could only stare, agonisingly aware that she was staring and mortified by the knowledge, but unable to tear her eyes away from him.

Abbie somehow managed to turn her back on those broad shoulders, lean hips and the strip of tautly muscled torso that beckoned to her through his unbuttoned shirt.

'You could have knocked or something,' she murmured, and was relieved that her voice sounded

normal—steady and composed. 'Given me some
warning that you were there . You scared at least a
year off my life.'

She was congratulating herself for having made
such a rapid recovery from what must have been an
episode of temporary insanity, when he suddenly
stepped up close behind her, bending slightly to peer
at her reflection in the medicine cabinet mirror. His
chest pressed lightly against her back, reminding her
that he still hadn't got around to buttoning his shirt.
His warm breath caressed her cheek. Abbie froze,
caught between panic and giddy exhilaration.

'You don't look like you've got a year to spare,' he
drawled close to her ear. 'Are you OK? You look a
little peaked.'

Peaked! An indignant shade of pink flared in
Abbie's cheeks, making a liar of him.

'I'm not wearing any make-up, that's all,' she said
stiffly.

'Ah, so that's it. You had me worried for a minute
there.' His tone was perfectly sober, but Abbie was
watching the reflected image of his narrowed eyes,
and she could have sworn she caught a glimmer of
laughter there.

His attention remained focused on her reflection,
his half-closed eyes subjecting her to a thorough
inspection from behind those unbelievably thick
lashes. His expression was solemn, slightly pensive,
giving no clue about what he was thinking. Abbie
endured his scrutiny in silence, her nerves stretched
as tight as piano wire. Finally he straightened and
took a step back.

'I guess you wear all that war paint to make yourself
look older,' he drawled. Abbie knew she hadn't
imagined the note of censure in his voice. Before she

could challenge it, or make any response at all, for that matter, he was half-way across the bedroom

She managed to hold her tongue until she was half-way down the narrow staircase.

'Be honest. If I'd come up to you in the bar looking like I do now, would you have even *considered* letting me drive the Shelby?'

Mal reached the bottom of the stairs just as she issued the challenge. He stopped and turned to face her. At first she thought he wasn't going to answer. Then a rueful grin slid across his mouth.

'Prob'ly not,' he admitted.

'Because without make-up I don't look old enough to drive a car, right?'

Pretending to give the question serious consideration, he took a minute or so to examine her from top to bottom, slowly and with evident enjoyment. His gaze lingered for several irritating seconds on the swell of her breasts. Abbie bit down hard on her indignation. By the time he lifted his eyes to hers again, she was wishing she had let the subject of how much make-up she should or shouldn't wear die a natural death.

'I guess that would depend on what part of you I was lookin' at,' he replied in a wickedly amused drawl. 'From the neck up, you could pass for sixteen or seventeen. But from the neck down——'

'We were talking about make-up,' she reminded him through stiff lips. 'Or war paint, as you so charmingly put it.' She didn't know what compelled her to pursue this ridiculous conversation. Unfortunately, the man seemed to have a knack for getting under her skin, arousing her fighting instincts.

'It's no big deal,' he said carelessly. 'I just think it's stupid to cover up such a pretty face with all that goop. Besides, it makes you look cheap.'

Abbie's jaw sagged in astonishment. Meanwhile, Malachi Garrett took advantage of her stunned silence to turn and walk away.

Abbie quickly recovered both her composure and the power of speech. *'Cheap!'* she yelped as she clattered down the last two steps. 'Is something wrong with my hearing, or did you just say I looked cheap?'

Mal's long legs continued to carry him down a narrow hall and toward the back of the house, leaving her to scurry along in his wake. 'That's what I said.'

'How dare you?' she stormed at his back. 'Of all the rude——' Angered as much by his blasé attitude as by what he'd said, she reached out and grabbed a fistful of his shirt-tail, yanking him to an abrupt half. 'Look at me when I'm talking to you, dammit!'

Mal pivoted to face her. His rugged face wore an expression of such innocent surprise that Abbie knew it had to be fake. She felt like slapping him silly; except she had a nasty suspicion that if she did he just might slap her back.

'What are you so worked up about?' he asked, still feigning surprise. 'I didn't mean for you to take it personally.'

'You didn't——! You don't seriously think you can tell somebody she looks *cheap*, for God's sake, and expect her not to take it personally! You meant it personally!'

He shook his head in denial. 'No, I didn't. I only meant that too much make-up makes any woman look cheap.' Abbie searched his face for some sign that he was amusing himself at her expense. She had just about decided to give him the benefit of the doubt when he added in a bland tone, 'Especially if she loads her eyelids down with three or four layers of purple gunk.'

Abbie sucked in a strangled breath. She felt hot colour surge up her neck and flood her face as she fought to hold on to her temper. It didn't help that Mal had finally allowed his sensuous mouth to curve in a devilish, taunting grin.

'You insufferable——' she began through clenched teeth.

'Ah-ah, no name-calling,' he interrupted. 'I was only getting back at you for saying I looked like a bum.'

Abbie glared at him. 'You did look like a bum.'

His bushy brows rose eloquently, but he refrained from making the obvious and expected response. His gaze dropped to her hand, which was still clutching the tail of his shirt. Abbie snatched it back as if she'd suddenly discovered that her fingers were curled around a slug.

'Y'know, it's really your own fault,' he drawled. Not waiting for a reply, he casually placed his hand at the small of her back and steered her through a doorway to their left.

Abbie swallowed nervously. She wasn't at all sure how to deal with this new Malachi Garrett. In the space of two or three minutes he seemed to have turned into a completely different person. If the idea hadn't been so preposterous, she might have suspected that he was flirting with her.

'What's my own fault?' she asked warily.

'That I get such a kick out of needling you. If it wasn't so easy to make you pop your cork, I prob'ly wouldn't be tempted to do it so often.'

'I do not "pop my cork",' Abbie told him in a starched tone. If she'd been flustered before, now she was totally confounded.

'Sure you do,' he contradicted. 'When I made that crack about purple eye-shadow, I wouldn't have been a bit surprised to see steam come out of your ears.'

Abbie decided to ignore that last remark. She had the uneasy feeling that, somewhere between his startling declaration that he hadn't expected her to come back to the farm and his insulting reference to her make-up, she'd missed something. Something important.

They passed through a small dining-room and into an enormous farmhouse kitchen equipped with every labour-saving device imaginable. Abbie came to a surprised halt just inside the room, causing Mal's chest to collide with her right shoulder. His arm instinctively curved around her waist, his hand closing on her hip for a second before he withdrew it.

The breath she had just inhaled seemed to snag on something in her throat. She could still feel the warm, firm, disturbingly erotic pressure of his fingers, even after he'd removed his hand. Frantic to hide her reaction to such a casual contact, she hastily stepped away from him.

Mal strolled past her and went to check the simmering contents of a large pot on the gleaming copper range. When he lifted the lid, Abbie caught a whiff of a rich, meaty aroma that made her mouth water.

'It smells done,' he said in the lazy drawl that Abbie had already decided was the sexiest voice she'd ever heard. 'The plates and bowls are in the cabinet above the dishwasher,' he added as he carried the stew-pot to a round, highly polished oak table at one end of the kitchen.

Abbie took her time collecting two ironstone plates and matching bowls from the cabinet, lecturing herself about maintaining her professional objectivity. Don't even think of him as a man, she told herself. He's just a story . . . possibly the biggest story you'll ever have a shot at. If you blow this chance, you'll regret it for the rest of your life.

Her resolve once more firmly in place, she turned toward the table where Mal was arranging place-mats, napkins and cutlery. He glanced up just as she started forward. The friendly smile that suddenly bared his strong white teeth transformed his stern features so completely that Abbie blinked in surprise. Who would have beileved that the creases in those lean cheeks had been hiding a pair of dimples? Abbie experienced a sinking feeling in the pit of her stomach. So much for professional objectivity, she thought in dismay. No way would she be able to think of this man as just another story.

When she was only a few feet from him, Mal's smile seemed to cool slightly, making her wonder if her expression had somehow betrayed her unsettling thoughts. She hastily pinned on a smile of her own. Except hers felt stiff and unnatural; more like a grimace, actually.

'I hope that tastes as good as it smells.'

Thankfully, her voice sounded more natural than her smile felt. The friendly warmth returned to Mal's eyes, replacing the thoughtful, almost speculative look that had been there a moment before. Abbie breathed a silent sigh of relief.

'So do I,' he drawled. 'My dad usually serves as chief cook and bottle-washer, but he took off for Florida last week to visit a friend.' A trace of cynicism shaded the word 'friend'. Abbie would have been willing to bet that his father's friend was female.

'You and your father live here together?'

'That's right.' He slanted her a wryly amused look as he took the plates and bowls from her hands. 'I suppose it's just as well he isn't here. He'd have taken one look at you, and I'd have had to find myself another driver.'

'I take it he's something of a ladies' man,' Abbie said cautiously.

'You could say that. You could also say that he's a randy old goat, which would be closer to the mark. Would you rather have beer, coffee or iced tea?'

'Tea, please,' she answered absently.

His comments about his father had roused her curiousity. But if she started asking questions that he considered too personal, he might retreat behind that tough, macho wall again. Still, she reminded herself, she was here to get a story . . .

'Are your parents divorced?'

She asked the question casually, as if she were only making small talk. Mal's answer was just as casual, ensuring that she was caught unprepared.

'No,' he murmured as he started back to the table. 'They never bothered to get married.'

He was looking straight at her when he said it. Abbie instinctively knew he expected her to be shocked. She *was* surprised, and she didn't try to hide it, but she neither blushed nor averted her eyes. His level gaze never wavered from her face.

'Stew's getting cold,' he said in the same matter-of-fact tone. Then, unexpectedly, he flashed a crooked, boyishly appealing grin. 'Sit down. If you promise not to fall asleep, I'll tell you the story of my life while we eat.'

Abbie dropped rather heavily into the chair. By the time Mal was seated at her right, she had managed to control her stunned reaction. Just my luck, she thought as he started ladling stew into her bowl. Malachi Garrett offers to tell me the story of his life, and here I sit without a tape recorder or a notebook.

CHAPTER FIVE

SILENCE followed Mal's last, astonishing remark. He must have been joking, Abbie decided as she opened her napkin and spread it on her lap. It would be expecting too much to believe he'd been serious.

She shifted her attention to the bowl of stew in front of her.

'This is delicious,' she declared in surprise when she'd swallowed the first rich, perfectly seasoned spoonful.

Mal sampled the stew. He looked a bit surprised himself. 'It's not half bad, is it?'

They ate in silence until the worst of Abbie's hunger had been satisfied. Back to business, she thought as she helped herself to more stew.

'So . . . when do I get to hear the story of your life?'

He slanted her a brief, enigmatic glance. 'Leave some room for desert.'

Was he trying to sidetrack her?

'I don't usually eat dessert. Have you always lived here?'

He stopped eating to frown at her. 'Don't tell me you're one of those idiotic females who's always on some kind of fad diet.' He sounded disgusted. 'Counting every calorie, afraid you'll gain five pounds and won't be able to stuff your behind into a pair of sixty-dollar designer jeans.'

Abbie patted her lips with the napkin before she answered. 'I've never dieted in my life. I don't often eat dessert because I don't happen to have a sweet tooth.

And how much I pay for a pair of jeans is nobody's business but my own.'

Garrett lifted his glass of tea in salute. '*Touché*,' he drawled. 'Have you always been so . . .?' He trailed off, frowning slightly. Abbie inferred that he was searching for just the right adjective.

'Outspoken?' she suggested. 'Assertive?'

'Assertive.' He repeated the word thoughtfully, testing it. The right side of his mouth lifted a centimetre, allowing her a brief glimpse of one dimple. 'Close enough.'

Close enough to what? Abbie wondered, but she didn't ask. 'Yes, I have always been assertive. And outspoken. I tend to say what's on my mind, and when I see something I want, I go after it.'

She expected him to make some response, probably sarcastic. Instead, he gazed at her solemnly for a few seconds, then merely nodded and started eating again. Abbie hadn't a clue about what he was thinking.

'You dislike assertive women, don't you?'

'I dislike self-centred, aggressive women,' he corrected as he reached for another slice of bread.

'And how would you define the difference between assertive and aggressive?' she asked casually.

Mal shrugged. 'You just described yourself as assertive. You say what's on your mind, and when you see something you want, you go after it. But you aren't the kind of woman who's determined to get what she wants at any cost. For instance, I can't see you using people who think of you as a friend. Or stabbing them in the back,' he added after a second's hesitation.

Abbie experienced a twinge of something that felt uncomfortably like guilt. Obviously, he credited her with possessing some scruples. She wondered what his opinion of her would be when he discovered that she was using him and the predicament he was in to get a story. She refused to dwell on the possibilities, telling herself that her Malachi Garrett exclusive was all that mattered.

'Did some woman do that to you?' she asked. 'Use you, or stab you in the back?'

He gave her a wry look. 'You can add blunt to assertive and outspoken.'

He didn't sound annoyed, and he hadn't told her to mind her own business. Abbie decided to press for an answer.

'Well?'

'And persistent,' Mal drawled. He laid his spoon on the plate beneath his bowl and sat back in his chair. Then he just looked at her.

He probably thought she would be intimidated by that unrelenting stare, and back off. If that was the case, he had another think coming. She stared right back at him.

'That's it, isn't it?' she challenged. 'Some woman used you or disappointed you in some way, and you haven't trusted a female since.' She waited for a reluctant admission that she was right.

'If you're sure you don't want dessert, have some more stew,' Mal suggested amiably.

She refused with an impatient shake of her head. 'No, thank you. You're not going to answer me, are you?'

She thought she saw a glimmer of amusement in his hooded eyes. Damn the man! Obviously the direct approach wasn't going to work with him. She could ask him questions till she was blue in the face, and he would simply ignore the ones he didn't want to answer. All right. She'd just have to switch tactics. She collected their dishes and cutlery and started carrying them to the sink. When Garrett realised what she was doing, he pushed his chair back from the table and came after her.

'You don't have to do that.'

Abbie sent a smile over her right shoulder as she placed the dishes on the counter next to the sink. 'I don't mind. You did the cooking.'

He looked surprised, but he didn't argue. He leaned against the counter and watched silently while she unbuttoned her cuffs and rolled up her shirt sleeves.

'Where's the washing-up liquid?' she asked, hoping to distract him.

Instead of answering, he stepped away from the counter and closed the distance between them in one smooth, gliding movement. Abbie instinctively tensed; for what, she wasn't sure. A second later his hands settled on her waist from behind.

'What——'

Before she could decide how to complete the question, he had moved her a couple of feet to the left and was squatting on the floor next to her right leg. His shoulder nudged her thigh as he opened the cabinet beneath the sink and took out a bottle of liquid detergent.

'Here you go.' His long frame unfolded and he stood beside her. Too close beside her. Abbie could feel the warmth of his body, smell the tangy scent of the shampoo he'd used. Then he removed a towel from the drawer he'd opened.

'I'll dry and put away.'

The offer surprised her. Then she remembered that he and his father were bachelors. She hadn't seen any evidence that a woman was or had recently been in residence, and he had referred to his father as the chief cook and bottle-washer. She wondered who was responsible for the other household chores. She couldn't imagine Malachi Garrett running a vacuum cleaner or sorting and folding laundry. They probably had a cleaning woman, someone who came in once or twice a week to change the sheets and tidy up after them.

Absorbed in her thoughts, she reached for the stack of dirty dishes and started to lower it into the suds. The next thing she knew, Mal's fingers were locking around her wrists. He carefully guided her hands back over the counter, then pulled them away from the stack of dishes.

'You almost scalded yourself,' he explained when Abbie stared at him in mute astonishment. 'The thermostat on the water heater is set for a hundred and fifty degrees.'

Her lips parted on a silent gasp. She had no way of knowing how tempting she looked at that moment—eyes opened wide in startled comprehension, full, soft lips parted invitingly. She was intensely aware that he hadn't released her wrists. His grip was firm enough to hold her when she made a half-hearted attempt to pull her hands free, but not so tight that it hurt. Abbie was fairly certain that he could feel her accelerated pulse. She made a second, more determined effort to tug out of his grasp. The pressure of his fingers increased slightly, letting her know that he wasn't ready to release her.

'Could I please have my hands back?' Her voice was a little shaky, and more than a little breathless.

'In a minute.' In contrast, Mal's voice was deep and alarmingly steady. His fingertips began to gently stroke the insides of her wrists. He couldn't have missed the way her pulse leapt in response.

'The dishes . . .'

'They aren't going anywhere.'

Her heart sank in dismay. He had suddenly switched to a husky murmur so sensual, so blatantly seductive, that certain areas of her body began to tingle with awareness.

As if he knew, he smiled into her eyes.

Abbie struggled to resist her strong physical response

to him, telling herself that to allow any kind of personal relationship to develop between them would be disastrous. She *must* remain objective!

His grip on her wrists suddenly went slack. She reluctantly acknowledged a twinge of disappointment, but before she could berate herself for not feeling relieved his hands slid up her arms and his fingers curled around her shoulders. Abbie stiffened in reaction to the unwanted thrill that shot through her. Mal seemed to hesitate, then one of his hands moved to her chin and gently lifted it. He frowned when he saw the distress in her eyes.

'Relax,' he said in a gruff murmur. 'I'm just going to conduct a little experiment. I promise it'll be quick and relatively painless.'

Abbie's eyes narrowed suspiciously. 'Experiment? What kind of ex——'

She didn't get to finish the question. His mouth closed on hers with a tenderness that took her completely by surprise. His lips were firm, yet gentle, asking for a response rather than demanding one. His hand released her chin so that his fingers could follow the line of her jaw to her ear, where they explored each curve, ridge and hollow with a thoroughness that sent shivers down her spine. Eventually he abandoned her ear, but Abbie's relief was short-lived, because the next instant his fingers burrowed into the hair at her nape and began to lightly massage her scalp. Meanwhile, his other arm slid around her shoulders, while he stepped forward and deliberately pressed his body against hers.

Her hands instinctively found their way inside his shirt. His muted growl of pleasure was all the encouragement she needed to wrap her arms around his waist.

Her fingers leisurely explored his back, lingering to examine the smooth ridges of his ribcage and the length of his spine. A small but annoyingly insistent part of her consciousness warned that this was madness, sheer lunacy; that she was risking everything.

Mal ended the kiss so abruptly that a soft moan of complaint slipped past Abbie's lips before she could stop it. One second they were wrapped around each other, and the next he was several feet away, reaching for the dishtowel. He looked perfectly composed, damn him—calm and in complete control. Abbie stared at him dazedly for a moment before she collected her wits and hastily turned back to the sink. Not trusting her voice, she didn't say anything.

'I get the feeling you didn't think much of my experiment,' Mal drawled.

Abbie stopped scrubbing long enough to give him a frosty glare and then returned her attention to the dishes. When she didn't respond to his remark, he heaved a sigh that sounded, to Abbie's ears, just a bit vexed. She gritted her teeth and shoved a bowl into his waiting hand.

'You were wrong, you know,' he murmured.

'About what?' she asked tersely.

'When you said I've never trusted a female since.'

He spoke in the same matter-of-fact tone he'd used when he told her his parents had never bothered to get married. Abbie instinctively knew that his show of nonchalance was a smoke-screen. And that casual 'since' had been a tacit confirmation that she'd been right about the woman in his past. Her interest quickened, but she didn't say anything. If she started talking, he might stop.

'I trust you, Abigail Prudence Kincaid,' he said in the same offhand tone. 'If I didn't, you wouldn't be driving me to Washington.'

Abbie was foolishly touched by the admission. She deliberately injected a trace of sarcasm into her reply to conceal the fact from him. 'You don't have much choice, though, do you? If you want to win this bet you've made, you have to trust me.'

A wry smile flitted across his mouth as he took the second bowl from her hand. 'True.'

His candour was a pleasant surprise. Abbie impulsively decided to press on. 'Who was she?'

She wasn't at all prepared for the indulgently amused look in his eyes as he leaned back against the counter and crossed one ankle over the other.

'Which one?'

Abbie floundered in confusion. 'What?'

'Which "she" do you mean?' he drawled with exaggerated patience.

'The one who caused you to have such a rotten attitude towards women,' she answered bluntly. 'Was it your mother?'

His lazy amusement vanished, to be replaced by what looked like genuine amazement. 'My mother? Why on earth would you think——? Oh, I see. You're wondering if I hate all women because my mother deserted me as an infant or something.'

The very thought of his mother deserting him made Abbie's throat feel tight. Her reply was a silent shrug as she rinsed a plate and passed it to his waiting hand.

Mal accepted it with a negative shake of his head. 'Sorry to disappoint you, but my mother isn't to blame for my rotten attitude towards women. And, to set the record straight, she didn't desert me or my father.'

Abbie refrained from asking any of the half-dozen questions that sprang to mind, not wanting to sound as if she were interrogating him.

'Both my parents have always been what you might call free spirits,' he said drily. 'They believe that the concept of marriage is contrary to the laws of nature.

Which is just as well, I suppose, since neither of them is emotionally equipped to maintain a monogamous relationship for more than a few months.'

He turned away to store the cutlery he'd been drying in a drawer. While he was doing that, Abbie took the dishcloth to the table and wiped up a few breadcrumbs. Seconds later Mal appeared at her side. He was holding a plastic container, into which he ladled what was left of the stew. He snapped a lid on the container, then picked it up and headed for the refrigerator.

'Don't bother to wash the pot,' he told her. 'Just run some water in it and let it soak.'

Abbie's teeth worried her bottom lip as she waited for the pot to fill with hot water. So far he'd told her just enough about his parents to stimulate her curiosity. She wanted to know more; a lot more. His childhood and adolescence must have been unorthodox, to say the least. The details of his formative years might even provide enough material for a separate article.

'Are you absolutely, positively sure you can't hold any dessert?'

Abbie glanced over her shoulder. Mal was standing in front of the open refrigerator, his right arm resting along the top of the door. Balanced on the palm of his left hand was a Sara Lee cheesecake.

'Well . . .'

A slow grin spread over his face. 'Why, Abigail Prudence, I do believe I've discovered your Achilles' heel.'

Abbie smiled sheepishly. 'If I didn't know better, I'd think you've been talking to my mother.'

His soft, throaty chuckle caused her breath to catch and goose-bumps to sprout on the back of her neck. Fortunately, he closed the refrigerator door and carried the cheesecake to the table, giving her a chance to regain her equilibrium.

'So you don't have a sweet tooth,' Mal drawled as he cut two large wedges of the rich dessert.

'Cheesecake isn't sweet,' she replied. 'Just fattening.'

He placed one of the wedges in front of her. 'And addictive,' he said gravely.

'Extremely addictive,' she agreed.

She waited several minutes before speaking again. She hoped that a period of companionable silence would make him more receptive. 'I'm curious about something,' she murmured when she'd finished off the last of her cheesecake. 'You said that neither of your parents is capable of maintaining a relationship for more than a few months. But they must have stayed together long enough to have you.'

Mal nodded. Her probing didn't seem to put him off. Abbie hadn't realised how tense she was until she felt her muscles relax.

'Dad had just turned thirty when they met,' he told her. 'That's the birthday that makes or breaks a lot of men. Suddenly it dawns on you that you've lived almost half your life. Even worse, you realise that your youth is behind you. You come face to face with your own mortality, possibly for the first time in your life.'

He paused, hooking an arm over the back of his chair and stretching his legs out under the table. 'Different men react differently. My father suddenly took it into his head that he wanted an heir, preferably a son. Liz had no desire to become a full-time mother, but she thought she should experience pregnancy and childbirth at least once in her life.'

Abbie stared at him, appalled. 'Are you saying she never intended to stay and raise you, or take you with her when she left your father?'

'That's right. They worked it all out before she got

pregnant: she'd stay here until after I was born. Dad would support her, make sure she had the best medical care, and when she was ready to leave he promised to give her enough money to get wherever she wanted to go and pay her rent for a year.'

Abbie was stunned, and she knew it showed. She shook her head as if to clear it. 'That's . . . incredible. I can't imagine how any woman could carry a baby for nine months, bring him into the world, and then just turn her back on him and walk away.'

'She didn't.'

Abbie shook her head again, this time in confusion. 'But you just said——'

'I told you how it was supposed to happen,' he interrupted. 'It didn't work out quite that way. Liz ended up staying a lot longer than she'd intended. She didn't leave for good until I was fourteen.'

'For good?' Abbie repeated in amazement. The more he told her, the more intrigued and fascinated she became. The Garretts had to be the strangest family she'd ever come across. Her fingers itched for a pen and notebook, so she could get all this down while her impressions were fresh. 'Do you mean she left more than once?' she asked incredulously.

Mal's soft laugh sounded more resigned than amused. 'She left and came back so many times that at one point Dad threatened to get a revolving door for his bedroom.'

'She must have cared about you both, though, if she kept coming back,' Abbie murmured.

'I suppose she did, and still does, in her own way. The trouble always was that she and Dad are too much alike. Neither of them is capable of making an emotional commitment.' A cynical smile flickered across his mouth. 'On the other hand, neither of them is cut out for a life of celibacy, either. The last time Liz came back, she found Dad——' He cut himself off in mid-sentence, cleared his throat, then drawled, 'Entertaining a female guest.'

Abbie stifled a smile. She wouldn't have expected him to censor his language for her ears. 'She actually caught them . . . er . . .'

'In the act.'

'What did she do?'

'Turned around and carried her suitcase back down the stairs and out the front door. She hasn't set foot on the farm since.'

'Can't say I blame her,' Abbie muttered.

Mal shrugged. 'It was only a matter of time till she caught him with somebody. Dad never could stand to be without female companionship for more than a few days. I've lost count of the number of women "friends" he's had over the years.'

Abbie gave him a shrewd look. 'Would it be safe to assume that some, if not all, of them are responsible for your dislike of self-centred, aggressive women?'

His lashes suddenly dropped to screen his eyes. 'Oh, yeah. It would definitely be safe to assume that.'

That reply was deliberately abrupt, letting her know that, while he didn't mind talking about his parents, he was unwilling to be as open about himself. But Abbie wasn't about to back off now, not when she'd finally started to make some progress. She rested her chin on her palm and gazed at him with unabashed curiosity.

'You did offer to tell me about yourself, you know. If you weren't serious, or you've changed your mind, all you have to do is say so. I promise I'll shut up and leave you alone.'

Her outburst didn't seem to faze him. He just watched her through narrowed eyes, his head tilted slightly to one side. 'Did you know that, when you get mad, your eyes change colour?'

'Dammit!' Abbie snapped in frustration.

She closed her eyes and drew a deep, calming breath, then released it in a rush. He had to be the most exasperating man she'd ever met. 'They do what?'

'Change colour. Normally they're sort of aquamarine, but when you get riled, they turn as green as jade.'

Abbie suspected that he was trying to provoke her again, so she didn't respond. A pensive frown settled on her forehead as she watched him. He made short work of washing and drying the dessert plates and utensils, performing the routine task as if he'd done it a thousand times. Maybe she'd been wrong about the cleaning woman.

When he'd finished putting everything away, he leaned back against the counter, arms folded over his chest. Abbie noticed that his hair had dried. She wondered if it felt as silky-soft as it looked in the glow from the overhead light. She also wondered what he was thinking as he regarded her so intently. She wondered, but she didn't ask. She had decided not to ask him any more personal questions . . . for the time being, anyway. She would back off for a while, give him some space. Lull him into a false sense of security.

Mal's voice interrupted her scheming.

'If you're really interested in my family history, we'll have plenty of time to cover it during the next couple of days. In the meantime, I have a favour to ask.'

He had dropped the phoney nonchalance, and there wasn't a trace of amusement—indulgent or otherwise—in his voice. Abbie was instantly on guard.

'A favour?' She knew she sounded a little suspicious. She didn't particularly care.

'Yes. When we go into town tomorrow, you'll meet another engineer who's also designed an experimental fuel-efficient engine. Naturally, I think my design is the better of the two.'

'Naturally.' Abbie unconsciously mimicked his drawl. 'And this bet you've made—I assume the purpose is to prove that fact to the other engineer?'

'Right. Both cars will leave the courthouse square at noon tomorrow. The winner will be the car that consumes the least amount of fuel and has the fewest mechanical problems during the trip.'

Abbie frowned at him. 'I thought this was going to be a race.'

'It is. Each of us will be trying to get to DC first, and we've set a deadline of noon, Monday. If either car hasn't made it to the Capital Building by then, it means an automatic forfeit.'

'Tomorrow's Saturday,' Abbie murmured. 'So you're allowing two days to make the trip. That should be plenty of time, shouldn't it?'

She thought Mal's smile looked a bit grim. 'It depends. Remember that both these engines are experimental. Up till now, all the testing's been done on a nice, safe, oval track, under controlled conditions.'

Abbie felt a twinge of unease. 'In other words, either or both of the engines might break down.'

He dismissed the suggestion with a shrug. 'Theoretically, anything could happen. But I'm not worried. Both the Shelby and my engine will go the distance.'

He seemed confident, she thought; and he should know. 'But what about the other car? Evidently you know the guy who designed the engine. How good is he?'

'She.' He ejected the word from his mouth as if he couldn't wait to be rid of it. Abbie wasn't sure she'd heard him correctly.

'I beg your pardon?'

'I said she,' he muttered. 'The engineer who designed the other engine is a woman.'

Abbie experienced a stunning burst of insight. Of course! The woman the waiter at the hotel had told her about—the one who'd jilted him, then used what he had taught her to steal his clients.

'We used to be lovers.' He revealed the information reluctantly, Abbie could tell. She prudently held her tongue. His lips twisted in a cynical facsimile of a smile as he added, 'Until she decided to head for greener pastures.'

Abbie bit her lower lip, hesitating briefly. 'If you don't mind my asking, what are the terms of your bet?'

She could see that the question had taken him by surprise. He'd probably expected her to ask something a lot more personal.

'If I win, she pays me twenty thousand dollars.'

Abbie's jaw dropped in astonishment. 'And if she wins?' she asked in a faint voice.

Mal closed his eyes, as if to shut out an unpleasant sight. 'I move to New York and become her partner.' He said it as if he were pronouncing his own death-sentence. His eyes opened. Their gazes locked. Abbie felt the impact of his formidable will, the force of his determination to win. A tiny shiver of excitement slithered down her spine.

'I've got a lot at stake here, Abigail Prudence,' he said softly. 'I'm counting on you. Don't let me down.'

She shook her head firmly. 'I won't.'

He nodded once, evidently satisfied with the response. 'Right. Now, about that favour.'

Abbie sat forward expectantly. 'Yes?'

'When we go into town tomorrow, I want you to pretend to be my lover.'

CHAPTER SIX

THE right front tyre of Deke's truck found another pothole. Abbie supposed she should be grateful that she wasn't bouncing around the cab like a ping-pong ball. She couldn't work up much gratitude, though, because Mal's left arm had her shackled to him so tightly that she couldn't have moved if she'd tried.

She didn't delude herself that he was holding her so close out of concern for her comfort. He was just making sure that Deke thought exactly what Mal wanted him to think. Judging by the knowing looks Deke kept sliding in her direction, the strategy was working. The complacent smile Mal couldn't quite wipe off his face told her that he thought so, too.

She was extremely irritated—mostly with herself, for having allowed Malachi Garrett to manipulate her into taking part in this crazy charade. Last night she had been so flabbergasted by the 'favour' he'd asked of her that she hadn't reacted for several seconds, which had proved to be more than enough time for the conniving devil to outfox her. He'd pretended to interpret her dumbfounded silence as assent. When she'd tried to set him straight, he'd merely smiled and told her not to worry, that he was sure she would give a convincing performance. And then he had neatly forestalled any further discussion by suggesting that they take the Shelby out so she could get in some more driving practice.

When she and Mal reached the garage, she discovered that the Shelby had been loaded on to a long, flat-bed trailer that was hitched to the rear bumper of Deke's truck. Deke was sitting patiently on a corner of the trailer. Apparently he'd been expecting them.

The three of them climbed into the truck and Deke towed the trailer over several miles of rutted gravel roads, until finally they reached one with a smooth asphalt surface. Mal backed the Shelby down a hinged ramp that Dake had lowered from the rear of the trailer. When he cut the car's engine and unfolded himself from behind the wheel, Abbie was waiting to take his place.

'Aren't you going to make me wear a helmet?' she asked as she started to step past him.

She was only teasing him a little, the way he'd been teasing her for the better part of the evening. She certainly wasn't prepared for his response. His left arm suddenly snaked around her waist and he pulled her against him, so hard that the breath left her lungs in a surprised whoosh. Abbie barely had time to register his wolfish grin before he planted a swift, hard kiss on her mouth.

'Maybe later,' he drawled when he released her. 'You could be in for a rough ride when we get back to the house.'

The outrageous remark was so unexpected that Abbie's only immediate reaction was a blank, open-mouthed stare. Mal took advantage of her shocked silence to hustle her into the driver's seat. By the time indignant outrage replaced her stunned disbelief, he had walked around the car and was climbing in on the opposite side.

'How *dare* you?'

Her voice throbbed with anger, but before she could unleash the full force of her wrath Mal suddenly leaned across the space between the black leather bucket seats. Abbie instantly stiffened, her spine pressed against the contoured backrest in instinctive withdrawal. When his hand lifted towards her shoulder she sucked in a sharp, alarmed breath and raised her own hand to slap it away.

'For God's sake,' he muttered under his breath. 'I was only reaching for your seat-belt.'

'I can fasten my own seat-belt,' she informed him curtly.

'Then do it!' he snarled. 'Deke's watching us like a hawk.'

'So what?' She had no intention of reaching for the shoulder-restraint until he had backed off. 'After that disgusting little scene you just improvised, he'll probably assume we're having a lovers' spat.'

Mal inhaled slowly, deeply. Abbie could almost feel the drain on his self-control as she silently counted to ten along with him.

'Fasten the damned seat-belt and start the engine,' he said in an ominously soft voice.

'I will.' She was careful to keep her own voice low as well. 'As soon as you're back on your side of the car.'

For a moment she thought she'd gone too far. His mouth thinned to a slash and the muscle along his jaw worked as if he were grinding his teeth. But then he suddenly shoved away from her. He had his own seat- and shoulder-restraints fastened while she was still wrestling with hers. As soon as they were underway, she said very clearly and distinctly, 'You were deliberately vulgar and insulting back there.'

He heaved a gusty sigh. 'You agreed to play the part, dammit.'

'Wrong!' she corrected. 'I never agreed to anything.'

'You didn't refuse, either,' Mal was quick to point out.

'Possibly because you didn't give me a chance to!'

He shifted restlessly. 'Yeah, well . . . I was afraid that if I gave you time to think about it, you'd say no.'

The gruff admission effectively spiked Abbie's growing resentment. She waited until she'd negotiated the forty-five-degree curve, then bluntly informed him that she expected an apology.

There was a second of surprised silence before Mal's indignant, 'For what?'

'You know perfectly well for what.'

'All I did was kiss you!'

Abbie took her eyes from the road long enough to give him a frosty glare.

'And make one slightly risqué remark,' he added grudgingly.

'If that was your idea of a "slightly risqué" remark, I hope I'm not around when you decide to be really offensive.'

Mal was silent for so long that she thought she'd managed to get in the last word. She was about to repeat her request for an apology, when he drawled, 'Abigail Prudence Kincaid, you're a perfect example of how deceptive appearances can be. You *look* like a warm-blooded, fun-loving woman.'

Abbie's fingers clenched on the steering wheel. 'Because I have blonde hair and curves in all the right places, you mean? How terribly disappointing it must be to discover I'm not the empty-headed bimbo you took me for.'

'That wasn't what I meant!' Mal snapped. 'Lord, I don't know why I even bother to talk to you.' He sounded fed up, as if he had reached the limit of his patience. 'We've gone far enough. Turn the car around and head back.'

Abbie felt a faint prickle of alarm. The road was too narrow for a U-turn, which meant that she had to back up a couple of times to get the Shelby pointed back in the direction they'd come. When she looked over her right shoulder to make sure she wasn't reversing straight into a ditch, she managed to sneak a quick glance at Mal's profile. What she saw caused her alarm to escalate.

The sight of a full moon threw his head and shoulders into stark relief. He was staring straight ahead, his posture rigidly erect. Angry tension emphasised the thrust of his jaw, while the full curve of his lower lip had all but disappeared.

'I'm sorry.' From the corner of her eye, she saw Mal's head swivel toward her in surprise. 'You're right—sometimes I do come on like the knee-jerk variety of feminist. It's a conditioned response, I guess.'

She could feel him watching her in the silence that followed her sincere, if reluctant, apology. She knew when his gaze traced the line of her nose, the curve of her jaw. She was aware of the exact instant when his attention shifted to her breasts. They responded as if he'd touched them with his fingertips, instead of his eyes. She was grateful for the darkness that concealed her erect nipples and the hot flush that accompanied them.

'A woman as good-looking as you probably has to put up with a lot of . . . bull.'

The quiet observation surprised Abbie. 'Close enough,' she murmured wryly.

'I guess after a while it starts to get to you.'

She sighed. 'Yes. I know I shouldn't let it, but it does. You'd be surprised how many Neanderthals are running around loose in this country.'

Mal's only reply was a non-committal grunt. Neither of them spoke again until after the Shelby had been reloaded on to the trailer, and then the conversation was limited to the car.

'There are some last-minute things I need to see to,' he told her. 'I may be here for quite a while yet. You might as well go on up to the house and get some sleep.'

'All right,' Abbie murmured, knowing full well that she wouldn't go to bed until she'd finished bringing her notes up to date. She started to turn toward the house, but something stopped her. Perhaps it was the way he was standing, his shoulders slightly hunched and his hands jammed deep into the pockets of his jeans. Purely on impulse, she asked, 'Is there anything I could do to help you get the car ready?'

Mal's expression went blank with surprise for a moment before a faint smile briefly touched his mouth. 'I appreciate the offer, but most of what's left to do falls into the category of fine-tuning. Besides, you probably won't get much rest during the next couple of days. You'd better grab a few hours' sleep while you can.'

Abbie felt oddly disappointed.

'OK,' she murmured. But when she started to leave for the second time, Mal suddenly clasped her arm to stop her.

'Wait.'

Abbie gave him a questioning look. She tried not to appear too hopeful.

He released her arm and stuck his hand back into the front pocket of his jeans. Abbie noted the creases that had reappeared between his heavy brows and the way his lips were slightly pursed. His hesitation couldn't have lasted more than ten or fifteen seconds, but, by the time he finally spoke, she had prepared herself for the worst.

'Listen, about what happened before . . . when I made that crack about the helmet. I guess I was out of line, but I want you to know that I never intended to insult or offend you.'

His level gaze never wavered. He seemed to expect some kind of response.

'I—er . . . well . . . actually, I wasn't all that insulted,' Abbie muttered, then added with wry honesty, 'Or offended. To tell the truth, I was more fed up than anything else.'

Mal nodded solemnly. 'Because of the way I manipulated you, you mean?'

Abbie opened her mouth to say yes, but just then Deke called out a question about the Shelby—something concerning an adjustment to the intake valves.

'I'll be there in a minute,' Mal called back. He didn't bother to look at Deke when he made the reply, so he wasn't aware that three of the mechanics had come out of the garage and were gathered around the car.

'Being fed up is something I can relate to,' he drawled as if there'd been no interruption. 'I don't like to be manipulated either. Look, I'll understand if you'd rather not do that favour I asked—no hard feelings, I won't carry a grudge or anything. But I would like to know what to expect when we go into town tomorrow, so I'd appreciate it if you'd give me an answer now.'

His willingness to admit that he'd been out of line surprised Abbie. The fact that he was making an effort to mend fences impressed her. She only hesitated a moment before giving him his answer.

'Yes,' she said softly. 'I'll do it.'

She couldn't help smiling a little at his startled expression. Obviously, he'd anticipated a definite 'no'. He recovered quickly, though, returning her smile as he offered his hand. Abbie started to take it, then changed her mind.

'We have an audience,' she murmured. 'Deke and three of your master mechanics.'

'They're watching us?'

'Avidly.'

'Great,' he muttered. 'That means Deke's been shooting his mouth off.'

The irony of the situation wasn't lost to Abbie. Not so many hours ago she had decided to make herself as sexless as possible, in the hope that he would start to think of her as just one of the guys. Yet now, here she was, deliberately stepping closer to him, preparing to give the men gathered around the car the impression that if she wasn't already his lover, she soon would be.

She placed her hands on the front of his shirt, looked him straight in the eye, and whispered, 'Kiss me.'

Mal stared at her as if he thought something had gone seriously wrong with his hearing. Abbie heaved a long-suffering sigh. 'If we want to be convincing when we meet your old flame tomorrow, we'd better get in a little more practice.'

His eyes narrowed in surprise, but a grin tugged at the corners of his mouth. 'Preferably in front of an audience,' he agreed as his arms slipped around her.

When his head began to descend, Abbie stretched up to meet him. His lips were firm, smooth and surprisingly cool. The thought flitted across her mind that pretending to be intensely attracted to this man wasn't going to require a great deal of acting talent. And then his tongue delicately traced the seam of her mouth, coaxing her lips to part for him, and she forgot she was only supposed to be pretending.

His right hand wandered down her back, lingered briefly at the waist of her jeans, then continued on and proceeded to snuggle her pelvis into the wider structure of his. Abbie's bones dissolved; her muscles turned to jelly. She sagged against him with a small, helpless moan. Mal responded with a hungry groan and a restrained thrust of his hips that sent heat surging through her veins. The fingers of his left hand raked through her hair, then closed on a fistful of curls. He tilted her head first left, then right, experimenting with different angles, his mouth and tongue constantly in motion, until Abbie couldn't remember a time when he hadn't been kissing her.

When he finally lifted his mouth from hers, her eyelids fluttered open to reveal passion-fogged eyes that had darkened to jade. Gradually, as her brain began to function again, she became aware of the heavy thud of her pulse and the shallow, rasping sound of her breathing. She was comforted somewhat by the fact that Mal was displaying symptoms identical to hers.

'I don't think we have to worry about being convincing,' he said. His voice was deeper than usual and undeniably husky.

'No,' Abbie agreed. Belatedly realising that her arms were still wound around his neck, she withdrew them and took a hasty, self-conscious step backward. Mal instantly released her.

'This . . .' he began, then broke off and ran an agitated hand through his hair. 'I wasn't expecting this.'

He sounded perturbed. Abbie's chin lifted a couple of centimetres. 'Neither was I.' She told herself that it wasn't an outright lie. True, she had felt a spark of electricity when he'd kissed her in the kitchen, but that kiss had been chaste compared to this one.

Mal's brows pushed together in a frown that looked slightly belligerent. 'This . . . chemistry, or whatever you want to call it, between us can't interfere with the race.'

'I agree,' Abbie said in a brisk, no-nonsense tone. 'It can't and it won't.' Her story had to come first, no matter how attracted she might be to her subject.

'We'll just have to . . .' He trailed off and made an

impatient gesture.

'Keep our hands off each other,' she supplied.

'Right. No touching if we can possibly avoid it.'

'And no more kissing,' she put in firmly.

Mal's gaze dropped to her mouth. 'God, yes,' he said hoarsely. 'No kissing, under any circumstances.'

Abbie started to concur, then suddenly remembered why she had asked him to kiss her this time. 'What about tomorrow morning?' she asked with an anxious frown.

Mal closed his eyes and swore under his breath. 'I forgot. All right, the moratorium on touching and kissing will begin as soon as the race has officially started.'

Abbie's frown remained in place. Did he actually believe that they could pretend to be lovers right up until they got into the car and started the race, and then suddenly switch off their emotions and become completely immune to each other?

'I don't know . . .' she murmured uncertainly.

His eyelids came down to screen the expression in his eyes. 'If you don't think you can handle it, say so now.'

The challenge pricked Abbie's pride. She dismissed her doubts with a negligent wave of her hand. 'I can handle it,' she told him. 'No problem.'

'Good. Then we've got a deal?'

'We've got a deal,' Abbie confirmed. She started to stick out her hand, then glanced over Mal's shoulder and quickly brought it back against her side.

'I assume our audience is still there,' he drawled.

'You assume right. I don't think they intend to leave until they're sure the show's over.'

'Well, hell,' he muttered in disgust. He bent his head to study the toes of his shoes, then looked up into her eyes. 'I'm going to have to kiss you one more time.'

He sounded as if he'd rather dive naked into a crate of razor blades.

'No hands!' Abbie warned as he leaned toward her.

Mal froze. His mouth tried to twitch into a grin before he got it under control. 'No hands,' he promised solemnly. 'Just one quick little goodnight peck.'

Abbie didn't trust the gleam in his eye, but he closed the last two inches of space between them before she could tell him so. The instant his mouth touched hers, she knew the kiss wasn't going to be just a goodnight peck. He might have intended it to be—though she had her doubts about that—but the current that arced between them was too powerful to deny or resist. When Mal felt it, he made a deep, guttural sound; a sound that was part hunger and part despair. A sound that sent shock-waves all the way to Abbie's toes. His lips suddenly hardened, the pressure of his mouth increased. He wasn't asking for a response this time, but demanding one.

Abbie held out against the demand as long as she could. But she was only human, and he was putting out enough heat to melt both polar ice caps. Her lips softened and parted, willingly moulding themselves to his. Fortunately, when his tongue stabbed past them to plunder and pillage, the shock jolted her back to her senses.

'No!' The word was little more than a gasp as she jerked away.

One of Mal's hands lifted towards her, but then he seemed to realise what he was doing and shoved it into his pocket.

'I'm going to the house.' Abbie intended to sound forceful and censorious. Unfortunately, her voice quavered as if she were about to burst into tears, which rather spoiled the effect.

'Good idea.' Mal's tone was curt, his expression dark and brooding.

As Abbie marched up the slight incline to the farmhouse, she berated herself for having behaved like such a simple-minded fool. It was one thing to help him out of the predicament his macho posturing in front of Deke had got him into, but quite another to let herself succumb to his potent sex appeal.

'Idiot!' she muttered as she slammed the front door behind her. 'Dunce. Boneheaded half-wit.'

She continued to hurl insults at herself while she paced the floor of her room. For the moment, at least, all her frustration and anger were directed at herself. *She* was the one who had agreed to go along with his insane idea.

She abruptly stopped pacing and sank down on the bed. Until now, she hadn't been particularly interested in knowing more about the woman, but all of a sudden she was eaten up with curiosity. Who was she? When and how had she and Mal met? How long had they been together? Had he been deeply, passionately in love with her?

That last thought brought with it a sharp, unexpected stab of pain. Abbie hastily rationalised that she would feel a pang of sympathy for anyone who had been treated so callously . . . even a dyed-in-the-wool chauvinist like Malachi Garrett. The woman's only importance was as his opponent in the upcoming race. The fact that she had once used him to further her own career and then ruthlessly discarded him was irrelevant.

And what about the fact that you intend to use him to further *your* career? her conscience slyly asked. Is that irrelevant, too?

CHAPTER SEVEN

ABBIE took advantage of a relatively smooth stretch of road to cautiously arch her back, attempting to ease her cramped muscles without drawing attention to herself. But of course Mal noticed. He transferred his left hand from her hip to the back of her neck and began to lightly massage it with the pads of his fingers.

'Gettin' a little stiff, sweetheart?'

The phoney solicitude in his lazy drawl made Abbie want to kick him in the shins. 'A little.'

She refused to look at him. She suspected he was grinning. If he was, she didn't want to know. He'd been doing a terrific job of needling her all morning.

It had started as soon as she came downstairs. Mal had taken one look at her conservative, buttoned-up shirt and squeaky clean face, and ordered her back up to her room to take off her bra and put on some make-up.

'Wear that sexy blouse you had on yesterday. And the pearls,' he'd added as an afterthought. Rather than begin the day with an argument, Abbie had turned around and headed back upstairs. When she was half-way through the dining-room, Mal yelled a reminder to use plenty of purple eyeshadow.

When she returned twenty minutes later, he had her stand in the middle of the kitchen floor while he walked around her, inspecting her appearance from head to toe.

'You'll do,' he pronounced when he was finished. 'Have a seat. Breakfast is ready.'

Breakfast had turned out to be a mountain of

sourdough pancakes, link sausages, hash brown potatoes, a pitcher of orange juice and a fresh-brewed pot of coffee.

'Surely you don't expect the two of us to eat all this,' Abbie said as she pulled out a chair.

Mal spared her an impatient look as he forked a stack of pancakes on to his plate. 'Once we start the race, I don't intend to stop till we reach St Louis. That's a long, hard drive. Either fill up now or go hungry later.'

She had considered telling him what he could do with his link sausages, then thought better of it. She studied him surreptitiously as she helped herself to four of them, as well as a couple of pancakes. Apparently he'd decided to pretend their little encounter down by the garage last night hadn't happened. That was fine with her. She didn't care to discuss it, either. The entire episode would be better forgotten.

Only she was finding it difficult, if not impossible, to forget how his kisses and caresses had felt, or how her traitorous body had responded to them. She hadn't slept well, and when she'd woken this morning it had been to blurred memories of disturbingly erotic dreams. She'd had a good long talk with herself while she bathed, reminding herself of her reason for being here and that it would be unforgivably stupid of her to give in to her physical attraction to Malachi Garrett.

She'd thought she had herself fairly well in hand . . . until she'd entered the kitchen and seen him standing at the stove, barefoot and shirtless. He'd been in the act of flipping a pancake, his right arm lifted slightly, his muscles well defined by the bright morning sunlight streaming through the windows. Abbie had stopped dead in her tracks, her mouth suddenly dry. She might have made a sound; she didn't know. Mal glanced over his shoulder at her, and the next thing she knew he was telling her to go back upstairs, take off her bra and for God's sake put on some make-up.

It was not exactly an auspicious beginning to the day. Unfortunately, things had gone downhill from there. Deke had arrived as they were finishing breakfast. His knowing smirk when he took in Mal's partial state of dress grated on Abbie's nerves, but a sharp look from Mal had convinced her to let it pass.

When they left the house for the garage, Deke had taken charge of Abbie's suitcase. He walked slightly ahead of her and Mal. Abbie thought he was probably embarrassed by the steamy looks Mal kept giving her and the way he was openly fondling her bottom. *She* was certainly embarrassed, not to mention annoyed as hell. She hadn't objected when he'd put his arm around her waist—she had agreed to go along with the charade, after all—but before they were ten feet from the front porch his hand had dropped several inches and was lightly stroking the curve of her hip. By the time they reached the garage, she was stiff with resentment and pink with mortification. Deke preceded them into the building. Abbie took advantage of his temporary absence to reach back and pluck Mal's hand away. He immediately replaced it.

'Stop that!' she said in a furious undertone.

His hand stayed right where it was. 'Settle down,' he growled. 'You agreed to play the part, remember.'

'And you agreed to keep your hands to yourself,' Abbie retorted. 'Remember?'

'*After* the race has started,' he reminded her. 'And I will, don't worry. As soon as we pull away from the courthouse square, your sexy little body will be strictly off limits. But until then, it's mine to do with as I damn well please.'

Abbie had nearly choked on her outrage as he yanked

open the door and shoved her through it. 'The hell it is!'

She'd caught a glimpse of Deke and several men dressed in white overalls standing about twenty feet away before Mal suddenly grasped her upper arms and spun her around.

'The hell it is,' he'd echoed, then hauled her against him and kissed her to prevent her from arguing. 'Put your arms around my neck,' he'd ordered against her stiff, uncooperative lips.

Abbie had glared at him defiantly.

'Do it, Abigail.'

His deep, rumbling voice had lost all trace of a drawl. He'd sounded determined, implacable . . . dangerous. Abbie had reluctantly lifted her arms and draped them loosely over his shoulders.

'You're despicable,' she'd hissed against his mouth.

'And you're still a pain in the ass,' he'd replied. 'Now kiss me, and look like you're enjoying it—use some body language, wiggle against me a little.'

Abbie had sucked in a sharp, incredulous breath. 'You're carrying this a little too far, Garrett. I never agreed to act like a slut.'

Mal's eyes had narrowed ominously. 'Do it,' he'd growled. 'Or so help me, I'll leave you in town and get Joey Bender to drive the Shelby to DC.'

Of course, she had given in. With an ultimatum like that, she'd had no choice. But she'd made sure he understood how much she resented being forced to demean herself in front of Deke and the others.

She'd spoken less than a dozen words to him since. Her stony silence didn't appear to effect Mal in the least, damn him.

When they arrived at the courthouse square, Abbie was astonished at the number of people who had already gathered. There were old men in bib overalls, women clutching the hands of young children, a few teenagers—who must have skipped school to be there—and several businessmen types in suits and ties. Even more astonishing, they all seemed to know Malachi Garrett. People started calling encouragement to him and wishing him luck as soon as he alighted from Deke's pick-up. He smiled and waved in acknowledgement, then turned back to the open door of the cab.

'We're on,' he murmured drily as his hands closed on Abbie's waist. The second her feet touched the pavement, he casually draped a possessive arm across her shoulders.

Abbie released a resigned sigh and just as casually slipped her own arm around his waist. 'Is she here?' she asked under her breath.

His eyes swept the crowd once from left to right. 'No. She's probably waiting to make an entrance.'

'Are you sure?' she asked with a frown. 'You barely looked.'

Mal started steering her towards the trailer. 'Believe me, I'd know if she was here.' Abbie glanced at him sharply. She'd never heard him use that tone before. He sounded sarcastic, mocking; yet she sensed that the mockery was directed at himself.

'I want you to back the Shelby off the trailer,' he said as they approached Deke, who was already lowering the ramp. 'We might as well make it clear from the start that you're the driver on this team.'

Abbie cast an apprehensive glance at the narrow ramp, but she didn't argue. She understood that this wasn't a spur-of-the-moment decision, and also that the matter wasn't being put to a vote.

'All right,' she murmured.

Some of her uncertainty must have come through in her voice, because Mal's arm gave her shoulders an encouraging squeeze before he grasped her firmly at the waist and hoisted her on to the trailer bed.

'Don't get yourself in a stew,' he drawled. 'I trust you not to demolish the car I've got two years and a half-million of my own money invested in.'

Abbie grimaced. She could have done without the reminder. 'Thanks for the vote of confidence.'

Mal grinned as he dug the keys to the Shelby out of his pocket and tossed them to her. And then he calmly turned his back on her and his half-million-dollar car and strolled over to the kerb, where several bystanders had assembled to admire the sleek black machine. Despite Abbie's misgivings, she didn't have any trouble backing the Shelby down the ramp. As soon as all four tyres were safely on the pavement, she cut the engine and climbed out of the car to join Mal.

She was instantly aware of a change in the mood of the crowd. There was an almost palpable tension in the air that hadn't been evident five minutes earlier, and the soft but noticeable buzz of several dozen murmuring voices—some curious, others excited, a few overtly hostile. The sound increased in volume as two new arrivals made their way towards the Shelby. So many people had gathered at the edge of the street that all Abbie could see of the advancing couple was a pair of dark, professionally styled heads. Her scalp suddenly tightened in premonition. She hurried to Mal's side and impulsively wound her arm around his waist. One of his brows formed a wry question mark as he laid his arm along her shoulders to complete the link. Evidently he hadn't noticed the newcomers.

Abbie only hesitated a moment. He shouldn't have to face the woman who had jilted him without some kind of warning, at least a few seconds to prepare himself. Guided purely by instinct, she laid the palm of her free hand against his cheek and stretched up to kiss him. Mal's response was equally instinctive. His arm instantly locked around her neck. What Abbie had intended as a ruse, a harmless bit of play-acting that would give her a chance to warn him without being overheard, became something else entirely when his mouth opened and claimed hot possession of hers.

She was caught unprepared for the sensations that suddenly assaulted her: the scrape of his nails against her scalp as his hand closed on a fistful of hair; the hard, unrelenting pressure of his lips; the smooth, wet glide of his tongue as it sought and found hers. The soft rasp of denim against denim as he insinuated his knee between her legs.

The kiss seemed to last an eternity. When Mal finally released her mouth, his eyes were glazed and unfocused, his breath a blast of moist heat against Abbie's forehead. She could feel his struggle for control in every taut line of his body. It was small consolation to know that the kiss had shaken him every bit as much as it had shaken her. She took a half-step backwards, desperately needing some space between them. She couldn't bring herself to look at the crowd, which had become suddenly, utterly silent. To her chagrin, Mal's arm remained hooked around her neck.

'I should have known you'd be the centre of attention, Malachi,' a smoky female voice drawled in amusement.

Abbie felt Mal's shock in the sudden tensing of his arm, but she doubted that anyone else was aware of his reaction to hearing that voice. He slowly turned his head to face the woman who had spoken. His eyes were hooded, his long lashes forming a protective screen.

'Hello, Roxie.'

Abbie gave him high marks for remaining cool under stress. He looked and sounded so casual and relaxed that he might have been greeting his sister. Then the name he'd used registered and her heart skipped a beat. Her eyes flew to the woman's face.

If not for Mal's restraining arm, Abbie might have darted into the crowd, or tried to crawl under the Shelby. Less than two yards away stood Roxanne Winston, famous—some might say infamous—female engineer, darling of the jet set, and former 'close companion' to one of Wall Street's most powerful investment bankers. Two years ago she had become an overnight celebrity, when she'd collaborated with a renowned cardiologist to develop a new artificial heart. Unfortunately, their design had proven unsuitable for the majority of potential patients, but twenty-six-year-old Roxanne Winston had quickly gone on to establish herself as the country's foremost female engineer-inventor.

Abbie knew all this because she had once interviewed Roxanne Winston. In person and at length. The interview had resulted in her first sale to a national news syndicate. She remembered the three hours she'd spent in Roxanne's plush apartment on Central Park East as clearly as if the interview had taken place that very morning.

Anxiety gnawed at Abbie's stomach. Would Roxanne recognise her? It had been almost two years since their one and only meeting. Roxanne must have given dozens of interviews to dozens of nameless, faceless reporters since then. Surely she wouldn't remember the brash, determined young woman who had conned her way past the building's doorman and shown up at her apartment one Sunday morning, unannounced and uninvited, to request an interview?

Abbie had been so preoccupied with her fear of imminent exposure that she hadn't been paying much attention to what was going on around her. She suddenly became aware that the muscles of Mal's arm were bulging against the back of her neck and that his body was positively rigid with tension. Coming face to face with his former lover must have upset him more than she'd thought.

The fierce surge of protectiveness Abbie felt surprised her. Usually she had no patience to spare for the frailty of the male ego, yet now she found herself instinctively moving closer to Mal, replacing her arm around his waist and reaching up to clasp the hand that hung over her right shoulder. Her actions, her posture, even the provocative glitter in her eyes, all telegraphed an unmistakable message to Roxanne Winston and every other female present.

The slight hardening of Roxanne's expression confirmed that she had received the message loud and clear. She hadn't spoken since she'd announced her presence with that cynically amused remark, but Abbie didn't have to speculate about what she was thinking or feeling. Antagonism was visible in every delicate feature of her classically beautiful face. Roxanne hadn't expected to have to share the limelight with another woman, and she was more than a little put out by the fact that apparently the other woman had already staked a claim on Malachi Garrett.

Resentment started to build in Abbie. She met Roxanne's cool, disapproving gaze boldly. Who did she think she was, anyway? If the rumours were true, she had walked out on Mal without a backward glance or a fare-thee-well. Had she expected to stroll back into his life as if nothing had happened? Had she actually thought it would be that easy?

Roxanne's husky alto brought her indignant thoughts to an abrupt halt. 'You haven't introduced us to your friend, Mal,' she pointed out with a saccharine smile.

His arm stayed around Abbie's neck as he made the introductions in a brusque, slightly impatient tone. 'Abigail Kincaid, this is Roxie Winston, the lady who designed the other engine.' He indicated the lean, handsome man standing to Roxanne's right with a curt nod. 'And this is Tony Ferris, who, I presume, will be driving Roxie's car to Washington.'

Abbie hastily stifled a gasp. Tony Ferris had been one of the two Formula One drivers Mal had mentioned to Deke at the hotel yesterday, when they were trying to come up with the names of people he might recruit to drive the Shelby.

'That's right, old buddy,' Tony said with a grin. 'And I'll bet you a hundred dollars here and now that we'll get there first.'

'You're on,' Mal drawled without a second's hesitation. 'What the hell are you doing here? I thought you'd be in Indianapolis all month.'

'Yeah, I thought so, too,' Tony said drily. 'But I rolled the Lotus during time trials the day before yesterday. Roxie heard about the crash on the news and called to see if I was still fit to drive, and if I was, whether I might be interested in taking on this little job for her.' He flashed another boyish grin. 'Naturally, when she told me who the competition was, I jumped at the chance.'

'Naturally,' Mal muttered. 'And are you fit to drive . . . all the way to DC?'

Roxanne answered the question before Tony could. 'I assure you, he's in perfect physical condition.' Her smoky voice and the sultry look she gave Tony implied that she had personally tested his strength and endurance. 'When do we get to meet your driver, Mal?'

'You just did.'

Roxanne's and Tony's heads simultaneously rotated forty-five degrees to the left, which made them look like a pair of preprogrammed robots. Their identical, almost comical expressions of astonishment added to the effect. Tony recovered first, smiling broadly as he stepped forward to offer Abbie his hand. She released Mal's long enough to give it a single firm shake.

'I'll be damned,' Tony said softly. 'It must be love.'

Abbie wasn't quite sure how to react to that. She turned to Mal for a cue, and was even more perplexed by the affectionate, almost tender smile on his lips and the unexpected warmth in his eyes. There was no doubt that that smile, that warmth was for her. She reminded herself, quite sternly, that he was only putting on an act for Roxanne's benefit. Unfortunately, knowing that didn't prevent her heart from performing a double somersault.

'Could be,' he said in the husky murmur that was even sexier than his drawl. His thumb started tracing lazy circles on her palm. 'What do you think, Abigail?'

Think? How was she supposed to remember to *breathe*, much less think, when his eyes were sending coded messages to hers and his voice had raised goosebumps all the way down her back and the light friction of his thumb was filling her head with all sorts of wildly erotic images? She made a fist to hold it still and drew a tremulous breath.

'I think its too soon to tell.' The lie came easily, but then she'd had a lot of practice at lying lately.

'How sweet,' Roxanne drawled. 'I must admit I'm surprised, though,' she added in the same world-weary tone. 'I used to beg you to let me drive the Shelby, but you wouldn't hear of it. You claimed it was a classic, much too valuable to entrust to an inexperienced driver.'

'That's right,' Mal replied flatly. 'It is.'

'And yet you're going to let your . . . friend——'

'Abigail,' he interrupted. He was still outwardly calm, but there was a distinct edge to his voice that Roxanne couldn't have missed. She hesitated a moment, then yielded with a tight, insincere smile.

'As I was saying, I'm a little surprised that you're prepared to let Abigail——' she deliberately gave the name a slightly mocking emphasis '—drive your precious Shelby all the way to Washington. She must have excellent qualifications.'

It irritated Abbie to have them discuss her as if she wasn't there, but she held her tongue. This was Mal's confrontation; she would let him handle it in his own way. He looked straight into Roxanne's eyes as he responded to the overt scepticism in her last statement.

'She's a top-notch driver,' he said softly. 'But she's driving the Shelby to Washington because she has something that's even more important than the ability to handle a high-performance car.'

Roxanne's right eyebrow rose a curious centimetre. 'And what might that be?'

Mal's slanting smile was hard, cold, almost grim. 'She has my trust.'

Two dull red splotches appeared on Roxanne's flawless ivory cheeks and she stiffened as if she'd been slapped. Abbie might have felt a twinge of compassion for the other woman, if she hadn't been so busy trying to conceal her own distress.

She has my trust.

Guilt churned in her stomach. She was sure it must be written all over her face, as well. It did no good whatsoever to tell herself that he had probably said it just to get at Roxanne.

She wished she could expunge the words from her

memory, conveniently forget that he'd said them or she'd heard them. Damn it, it was too late to start having second thoughts. She was committed both to the race and to the story. Besides, as she'd pointed out to Mal last night, he *had* to trust her if he wanted a shot at winning the bet. It wasn't as if he had a choice, as if his trust had been given willingly.

Thankfully, no one seemed to be aware of the battle Abbie was waging with her conscience. 'I hate to break up the reunion,' Tony said into the strained silence. 'But it's almost eleven, and there are one or two things we need to go over before we take this show on the road.'

'Right,' Mal said tersely. He glanced past Tony to the crowd. 'How about moving over to Gladys's? We'd have a little more privacy there.'

'Good idea,' Tony agreed. 'I could go for a cup of coffee and a slice of Gladys's rhubarb pie.'

Roxanne had been as stiff and silent as a totem pole since her last exchange with Mal, but when Tony stepped off the kerb she suddenly came back to life. 'Just a minute, Tony.' The tone she used made it an order rather than a request. Tony's eyes narrowed with displeasure as he stopped and looked back at her in question.

'I'd prefer not to leave the car on the other side of the square while we have this meeting.'

During the pause before Tony responded, Abbie wondered if he was considering telling Roxanne to move the car herself. Despite his easygoing temperament, he didn't strike her as a man who was accustomed to taking orders. But he must have decided the four of them had already given the crowd of spectators enough to gossip about, because he merely shrugged.

'Fine. I'll bring it round and park it next to the Shelby, then we can keep an eye on both cars from the café.'

Abbie noticed as the other couple headed back across the courthouse square that Tony's right hand had a firm grip on Roxanne's arm and his head was bent close to hers, his mouth almost touching her ear. She'd have given a lot to know what he was saying. She left her arm around Mal's waist and let him steer her toward Gladys's Café, which was directly across the street. She didn't try to make conversation, because she had no idea what might pop out of her mouth once she opened it. Her conscience was still sniping at her, urging her to confess all before it was too late, despite her urgent pleas for it to shut up and let her get on with her job. When Mal uttered a soft, heartfelt 'Bitch!' half-way across the street, her heart lurched in alarm.

CHAPTER EIGHT

'I BEG your pardon?' Abbie said in a small, timorous voice.

Mal frowned impatiently. 'Not you, for pity's sake.'

The breath wheezed out of her in relief. 'Oh. Roxie.'

'Yeah. Oh, Roxie.' They reached the café and he released her to open the door. Abbie hurried through it ahead of him. If she moved fast enough, maybe she could avoid any more physical contact with him for a while. Her entire nervous system could use a few minutes' rest.

'Is this booth all right?' She was already sliding on to one of the black-vinyl-upholstered benches as she asked.

Mal gave her an odd look. 'Fine.' Instead of taking a seat on the opposite bench, he slid in beside her. His hip collided gently with hers. Abbie hastily scooted over against the wall.

'Get back over here,' Mal said in a muted growl. He gave her all of two seconds to comply, then shoved his arm behind her and clamped his hand on her waist to haul her back against him.

Abbie silently cursed the slick vinyl as her bottom slid across it. She could feel Mal's puzzled, questioning gaze, but she refused to meet his eyes, and tried to block out the warm fingers that were lightly, almost absently, caressing her waist.

'What's with you, anyway?' he muttered. 'You're stiff as a board.'

'I'm getting a tension headache.'

Which, if it fell short of being an explanation, at least

wasn't another bald-faced lie. Tension had been accumulating inside her for the past eighteen hours. The shock of meeting Roxanne Winston alone would have been enough to precipitate a lulu of a headache. Dear lord, if the woman had recognised her . . .

She didn't complete the thought, because Mal's hand suddenly moved from her waist to her nape.

'Here?' he murmured. His thumb found the hollow at the base of her skull and his fingers splayed over the muscle connecting her neck to her shoulder. He began a gentle, rhythmic massage that jump-started her libido and had her breathing shallowly through her mouth within seconds.

'Try to relax,' he coaxed softly. 'I know you're not crazy about this situation, but we only have to keep up the act for another hour.'

Abbie smiled.

He said said soberly, 'You don't like lying, do you . . . pretending to be something you're not?'

Abbie closed her eyes and wished she could believe that the sudden pain beneath her breastbone was caused by the sausages she'd had for breakfast. 'No,' she said huskily. 'I don't.'

The warmth of Mal's breath against her cheek alerted her to the fact that he was much closer than he had been a moment before. She kept her eyes closed, afraid that if she opened them he would see her guilt and confusion. She wasn't expecting the feather-light touch of his lips at her temple. Her breath caught audibly. She knew Mal had heard the small sound, because he suddenly went very still. His fingers stopped massaging in mid-stroke. She thought that for a second or two he even stopped breathing.

'I knew you were trouble the second I laid eyes on you,' he murmured. He sounded resentful. 'Dammit, Abigail!

How am I supposed to concentrate on this race, when every time I look at you I want to touch you, and every time I touch you I want to take you to bed?'

Her weakened resolve was miraculously restored to full strength. 'Simple,' she said coolly. 'Look, but don't touch.'

His left eyebrow rose in sardonic amusement. 'Easier said than done, I'm afraid.'

He leaned toward her as if he intended to prove his point. Abbie pressed her lips together and twisted her head away.

'Don't,' she murmured. Her voice was husky, but firm.

Mal's hand rested on her neck a moment longer before he removed it. Abbie relaxed a little, but she knew the reprieve was only temporary. The chemistry between them was too potent to be harnessed indefinitely.

She was thankful that Mal was no longer touching her. If he had been, he'd have felt the shiver that raced down her spine, and she had no doubt at all that he'd have instantly recognised the sexual excitement that triggered it.

The waitress finally came out from behind the counter to bring them two glasses of iced water. She didn't bother to conceal her curiosity, giving Abbie a thorough inspection while she removed an order pad from the pocket of her apron and a pencil from the frizzy salt and pepper hair above her ear.

'Mornin', Mal,' she drawled. 'What'll you have?'

Mal grinned and lifted a hand to the bill of his cap, pushing it back on his head. 'Four coffees, three slices of rhubarb pie and some aspirin for the lady, thanks, Irma.'

Irma wrote the order on her pad, then turned her sharp, inquisitive gaze on Abbie again as she stuck the pencil back in her hair. 'Headache?' she asked succinctly.

Abbie nodded. 'Yes.'

The more
you love romance . . .
the more
you'll love this offer

Mail this heart today! (See inside)

Join us on a Harlequin Honeymoon
and we'll give you
4 free books
A free bracelet watch
And a free mystery gift

308 CIH U11DP (C-H-P-09/89)

IT'S A
HARLEQUIN HONEYMOON—
A SWEETHEART
OF A FREE OFFER!
HERE'S WHAT YOU GET:

1. **Four New Harlequin Presents® Novels—FREE!**
Take a Harlequin Honeymoon with your four exciting
romances—yours FREE from Harlequin Reader Service®. Each
of these hot-off-the-press novels brings you the passion and tenderness of today's greatest love stories...your free passports to
bright new worlds of love and foreign adventure.

2. **A Lovely Bracelet Watch—FREE!**
You'll love your elegant bracelet watch—this classic LCD quartz
watch is a perfect expression of your style and good taste—and it
is yours FREE as an added thanks for giving our Reader Service
a try.

3. **An Exciting Mystery Bonus—FREE!**
You'll be thrilled with this surprise gift. It is elegant as well as
practical.

4. **Money-Saving Home Delivery!**
Join Harlequin Reader Service® and enjoy the convenience of
previewing eight new books every month delivered right to your
home. Each book is yours for only $2.24*—26¢ less per book than
the cover price—plus only 89¢ postage and handling for the entire shipment! Great savings plus total convenience add up to a
sweetheart of a deal for you! If you're not completely satisfied,
you may cancel at any time, for any reason, simply by sending us
a note or shipping statement marked ''cancel'' or by returning any
shipment to us at our cost.

5. **Free Insiders' Newsletter**
It's *heart to heart*®, the indispensible insiders' look at our most
popular writers, upcoming books, comments from readers and
much more!

6. **More Surprise Gifts**
Because our home subscribers are our most valued readers, when
you join the Harlequin Reader Service®, we'll be sending you additional free gifts from time to time—as a token of our
appreciation.

START YOUR HARLEQUIN HONEYMOON TODAY—JUST
COMPLETE, DETACH AND MAIL YOUR FREE-OFFER CARD

*Terms and prices subject to change without notice.
© 1989 HARLEQUIN ENTERPRISES LTD.

Get your fabulous gifts
ABSOLUTELY FREE!

MAIL THIS CARD TODAY.

PLACE
HEART STICKER
HERE

GIVE YOUR HEART TO HARLEQUIN

YES! Please send me my four Harlequin Presents® novels FREE, along with my free bracelet watch and free mystery gift. I wish to receive all the benefits of the Harlequin Reader Service® as explained on the opposite page.

NAME _____
(PLEASE PRINT)

ADDRESS _____ APT. _____

CITY _____ PROV. _____

POSTAL CODE _____   308 CIH U1DP (C-H-P-09/89)

OFFER LIMITED TO ONE PER HOUSEHOLD AND NOT VALID TO CURRENT HARLEQUIN PRESENTS® SUBSCRIBERS. ALL ORDERS SUBJECT TO APPROVAL.

HARLEQUIN READER SERVICE® "NO RISK" GUARANTEE

—There's no obligation to buy—and the free books and gifts remain yours to keep.
—You pay the low members-only discount price and receive books before they appear in stores.
—You may end your subscription anytime by sending us a note or shipping statement marked "cancel" or by returning any unopened shipment to us at our cost.

PRINTED IN U.S.A.
© 1989 HARLEQUIN ENTERPRISES LIMITED

308 CIH U1DP (C-H-P-09/89)

START YOUR
HARLEQUIN HONEYMOON TODAY.
JUST COMPLETE, DETACH AND MAIL YOUR
FREE OFFER CARD.

If offer card is missing, write to: Harlequin Reader Service® P.O. Box 609
Fort Erie, Ontario L2A 5X3

**Business
Reply Mail**

No Postage Stamp
Necessary if Mailed
in Canada

Postage will be paid by

Harlequin Reader Service
PO BOX 609
FORT ERIE, ONTARIO
L2A 9Z9

Canada Post
125
Postes Canada

'Not surprisin',' Irma observed. 'I saw you back that black monster of Mal's off the trailer. I guess you'll be drivin' it in this race.'

Abbie had to smile a little at the woman's directness. 'That's right.'

Irma's head bobbed in satisfaction. 'Figured as much. I'd better get you somethin' for an upset stomach, while I'm at it.'

When Irma had disappeared through a door that Abbie presumed led to the kitchen, she turned to Mal with a wry smile. 'She must know you pretty well.'

'Since I was knee-high to a grasshopper,' he confirmed. 'Irma and her sister Gladys operate what you might call an information clearing-house. Either of them could give you the address, phone number, birth date and present marital status of anyone born in this county in the last thirty years.'

Abbie was thinking it was a shame she hadn't known about the sisters a few days earlier, when the door at the front of the café opened and Tony and Roxanne entered. Irma reappeared just as they reached the booth. As soon as the other couple was seated, she placed a cup and a saucer before each of them and began filling the cups with coffee.

'Good to see you, Tony,' she said as she handed Abbie a small tin of aspirin. 'Still take it black?'

Abbie couldn't help noticing that Irma pointedly ignored Roxanne Winston. Judging by the slight compression of Roxanne's lips, she had noticed, too.

'Affirmative,' Tony replied. 'You never forget a thing, do you, Irma?'

Irma's gaze momentarily swung to Roxanne, who had picked up her cup for a dainty sip. 'That's right.'

The animosity that had suddenly invaded Irma's voice surprised Abbie. She was even more surprised by the friendly smile Irma gave her as she placed a dessert plate beside her saucer. Abbie frowned at the wedge-shaped object on the plate as if she wasn't quite sure what it was or what she was expected to do with it.

'Rhubarb pie,' Mal said in amusement. 'The idea is to eat it.'

Abbie shot him a mildly annoyed look. Since he hadn't asked if she wanted any pie, she had assumed the third slice he'd ordered was for Roxanne. She shook her head dubiously as she removed two aspirin from the tin. 'I don't think . . .'

'Go ahead, dig in,' Tony encouraged. 'It tastes better than it looks, honest.'

Unconvinced, Abbie turned to Roxanne. 'Have you ever tried it?'

'Once.'

The one-word answer and the faint grimace that accompanied it made it clear that once had been enough. Something inside Abbie tightened in response to Roxanne's bored, supercilious tone. She picked up her fork, determined to polish off every last crumb. Fortunately, Tony had been right—rhubarb pie did taste better than it looked.

'Not bad,' she admitted when she'd washed down the last bite with a sip of coffee. 'But I don't think it'll ever replace cheesecake as my all-time favourite dessert.'

Mal's mouth tilted in one of his sexy-as-sin half-smiles, and he lifted his hand to rub a lazy fingertip over her lower lip. The casual contact sent a jolt of electricity all the way to the soles of Abbie's feet, as she watched him transfer the finger to his own mouth.

'Slob,' he said softly. His tongue came out to lick an invisible dab of rhubarb pie filling from the end of his finger. Abbie's toes curled inside her shoes.

'Next time, use a napkin.' His voice was teasing, affectionately amused. His finger made another trip to her mouth, concentrating on the corners this time. It was still wet from his tongue. Abbie wondered with a touch of hysteria how she was going to get through the next two days with her sanity intact.

'On second thoughts, don't bother,' he said in that same teasing murmur. 'This way's more fun.'

The logical, rational part of her brain realised that this erotic little scene was being staged for Roxanne's benefit, that he was only playing a part. The trouble was, it was damned hard to be logical or rational when the mere brush of his finger against her mouth liquefied her bones and sent her heart into a tailspin. He seemed to hesitate, as if he were considering how much more improvisation was called for. A second later his open mouth covered hers. The kiss was blessedly brief, but devastating all the same. His tongue made a leisurely pass across the tender flesh inside her lower lip just before he abruptly pulled back. Abbie was dimly aware of swaying toward him. His arm instantly slipped around her and tucked her close against his side. So close that she could feel each disturbed thud of his heart through his ribcage.

'If you two have finished . . .' Roxanne's caustic voice brought Abbie plummeting back to earth.

'Finished?' Mal said in a lazily amused drawl. 'Not by a long shot. Maybe in forty or fifty years.'

Abbie reached for her coffee-cup to wet her parched mouth and throat. Forty or fifty *years*?

'Sounds like you've got it bad,' Tony remarked.

Mal glanced at Abbie. His tender smile made her extremely nervous. 'You could say that,' he murmured. 'I intend to marry her.'

Twenty minutes later Abbie leaned against the Shelby's right front fender while she waited for Mal and Deke to run a couple of last-minute errands. She narrowed her eyes, her attention drawn to the vehicle Tony had parked beside the Shelby.

Roxanne Winston's car. The one equipped with the experimental engine Roxanne Winston had designed. A brand new Mercury Sable. The pristine white paint contrasted conspicuously with the Shelby's midnight black; also with the scarlet upholstery visible through the Sable's tinted windows. Roxanne's car was an extension of its owner: sleek, sophisticated, stylishly contemporary. Beside it the Shelby looked like an anachronism . . . a hulking, lumpish machine that had somehow been transported from a less civilised age, when brute power had been prized above graceful lines and the efficient use of aerodynamics.

Abbie didn't like Roxanne's car. She didn't like Roxanne either, for that matter. Both the vehicle and the woman were too flawless, too slickly packaged, too . . .

Too perfect, damn it. The Shelby didn't stand a chance against such a superbly designed and engineered car. Mal had told her that he'd kept the original fuel-guzzling four-twenty-eight engine. No matter what modifications he'd made to it, Abbie didn't see how the Shelby could possibly consume less fuel than the Sable.

He was going to lose the bet.

The thought caused a cramping sensation in the general region of her heart. There was no point in lying to herself about the cause of her distress. If Mal lost the bet, he would have to move to New York and become Roxanne's partner. And Abbie didn't believe for a second that Roxanne would be content with merely a professional relationship. She wanted him back, and she meant to have him . . . on her terms.

That fact had been glaringly obvious when Mal had said he intended to marry Abbie. Tony's expression had reflected his stunned amazement. Roxanne, on the other hand, had looked positively furious. Abbie vividly remembered the antipathy in the other woman's cold blue eyes as they'd pinned her to the vinyl bench.

Resentful anger had surged inside Abbie, filling her chest and pushing up into her throat. It still amazed and annoyed her that Mal had appeared to be blissfully ignorant of the charged atmosphere around the table.

When he started hashing out the rules with Tony and Roxanne, the trio had quickly established a list of three simple, straightforward rules. Number one: a log was to be kept of each car's fuel consumption. The log would also include a record of any repairs made during the trip and the reason for each. Number two: each team was free to take whatever route they chose. And number three: observance of posted speed limits was optional. It was the extra condition Mal had insisted on including that had caused a knot of dread to form in Abbie's stomach.

Actually, it hadn't been a condition, so much as an ultimatum. It had also been the last in a series of unsettling surprises. First, Abbie had discovered that the race had been Roxanne's brainchild, not Mal's, as she'd assumed. She was still trying to decide how that fact would affect her story when Roxanne informed Mal that she had conceived the idea as a way to promote their individual research—something she had neglected to mention until minutes before the race was to start. To say that Mal had reacted negatively would have been a colossal understatement.

'Forget it,' he told Roxanne bluntly. 'If you think I'll let you turn this into a cheap publicity stunt, you've got another think coming. You'll have to come up with some other gimmick to get your picture on the cover of *Newsweek*.'

Roxanne had bristled defensively. 'There's nothing

wrong with wanting to be recognised for the work I've done. Unlike you, I appreciate the value of good publicity.'

'There's no such thing,' Mal retorted.

Roxanne flicked one elegant hand in an exasperated gesture. 'The Press isn't your enemy, Malachi. You may not want to admit it, but you need them as much as they need you.'

Mal shook his head, his expression obstinate. 'Nobody *needs* reporters.' Abbie controlled an urge to cringe. 'Hell, they're no better than scavengers. No, on second thoughts, they're worse than scavengers. They're parasites.'

Roxanne's expression had hardened noticeably. 'I want Press coverage of the race, Malachi.'

'And I don't.'

The silence following Mal's soft rejoinder could have been cut with a knife. He had deliberately let it stretch out until Roxanne began to look a little uneasy. Not worried, exactly, just slightly less confident than she had been.

'So where does that leave us?' she asked.

Mal had made her wait a few more seconds before he answered. 'It depends,' he said in a deceptively mild tone. 'If you've already made arrangements for one of your reporter friends to cover the race, all deals are off.'

The flush that had tinted Roxanne's creamy cheeks verified that she had done exactly that. Abbie had to give her points for perseverance and ingenuity, though. After only a second's hesitation, Roxanne had offered to call the editor she'd promised the story to and tell him the race had been cancelled . . . if, in return, Mal would agree to a joint Press conference when they reached Washington. He hadn't liked the idea, but Roxanne had eventually persuaded him that the deal she was offering was a fair trade-off.

'But get this straight,' he'd warned, and the hard glint in his eyes had served notice that he meant what he said. 'If I spot anybody dogging us who even *looks* like a reporter, I'll turn the Shelby around and head for home. End of race. And no race, no story.'

Abbie dug her hand inside her shoulder bag and fished around until she located the bottle of antacid tablets Irma had handed her as she left the café. It hadn't even occurred to Abbie to tell Irma she didn't need them. She had accepted the bottle gratefully.

'No charge,' Irma had said when she'd taken out her wallet. 'Consider it my contribution to helpin' you win the race.' After a quick glance to make sure Mal wasn't within earshot, she added under her breath, 'Take my advice, honey, don't let him bully you or boss you around. He'll prob'ly try, but you just keep in mind that his bark's worse than his bite, and give as good as you get.'

His bark's worse than his bite.

First Deke, and now Irma, had used that phrase to describe Mal. Abbie thought that, under normal circumstances, they were probably right. Unfortunately for her, these weren't normal circumstances. Try as she might, she couldn't forget his contemptuous denunciation of reporters. Scavengers, he'd labelled them. Parasites. *Parasites*, for God's sake! When he found out who she was and why she'd bamboozled him into letting her drive the Shelby . . .

She tipped the bottle and shook two antacid tablets into her palm. It irritated her that her hands trembled slightly. It annoyed her even more to acknowledge that Mal's derogatory remarks had stung, more than they should have. She tried to dismiss her reaction as a simple case of offended pride, but in her heart she knew it went deeper than that. The miserable, obnoxious truth was that his opinion had the power to hurt her. It wasn't enough that he'd given her his trust. Fool that she was, she had wanted his respect, too.

'Fat chance,' she muttered around the chalky tablets as she stuffed the bottle back in her bag. Considering how she'd deceived him, she would consider herself lucky if he didn't toss her from the top of the Washington Monument.

'Talking to yourself, Abigail?'

Abbie almost choked on the tablets. She spun around and levelled an accusing scowl at him. 'It would've served you right if I'd dropped dead of a heart attack. Then you'd have been stuck without a driver.'

Mal's stance was relaxed, his hands tucked into the back pockets of his jeans. His crooked grin had a predictable effect on her heart-rate. 'I could always get Joey Bender.'

The lazy taunt was the last straw. Abbie felt her self-control begin to slip away and didn't give a damn. 'Good idea,' she said curtly.

She dug the keys to the Shelby out of her purse and started around the car, intending to collect her suitcase. Mal didn't react until the hatchback popped open and the top half of her body disappeared into the storage compartment. Then he moved, covering the distance between them in three long strides.

'What the hell are you doing?' he growled over her shoulder.

Abbie gritted her teeth and vowed not to make a scene. 'What does it look as if I'm doing?'

Her fingers closed around the handle of her suitcase. A second later Mal's hand clamped over hers.

'It looks like you're going back on your word.'

Abbie cast an anxious glance at the Sable, even though the muttered accusation couldn't have carried more than a few feet. To her relief, she saw that Roxanne and Tony were still huddled over a road map they'd unfolded on the car's hood.

'Well?' Mal prompted impatiently. 'Say something, dammit!'

Abbie released the suitcase and yanked her hand from beneath his. He was too close, crowding her, his chest nudging her arm and each exhalation a warm caress against her cheek. She started to back out of the car. Before her shoulders had cleared the opening, Mal's hands clamped on her waist. The next thing she knew, she was sitting on the floor of the storage area, her legs dangling over the rear bumper. She glared up at him.

'Talk to me, Abigail.'

The gentle concern in his voice was Abbie's undoing. If he'd been his usual rude, overbearing self, she might have been able to stick to her impulsive decision to cancel their agreement. It would have been cowardly and unprofessional of her, and heaven knew how she would have explained to Roger, but at least she'd have been off the hook. No more lies, no more deceit. No more guilt. If she didn't take part in the race, she couldn't very well write a feature article about it, now could she? It had seemed the perfect solution . . . for her.

But what about Mal? How could she back out of their deal, when she knew that to do so would leave him without a competent driver and virtually assure that Roxanne would win their bet?

When she didn't say anything, he slipped a hand under her chin and lifted it so that he could look into her troubled eyes. 'Don't do it, Abigail,' he said softly. 'I knew you're upset, and probably madder than a wet hen, but don't get back at me by leaving me in the lurch. I need you.'

The simple, quietly spoken appeal sealed Abbie's fate,

and she knew it. Still, her instinct for self-preservation compelled her to make a half-hearted attempt to forestall the inevitable.

'You could always get Joey Bender,' she said peevishly.

Mal's head moved in a firm negative. 'Out of the question. It's you or nobody.'

The corners of her mouth indented wryly. Joey Bender had been her one and only trump card. 'Since you put it that way, I guess I don't have much——'

She abruptly cut herself off, her eyes narrowing to slits. 'Wait a minute. When we were in the garage this morning, you threatened to leave me in town and get Joey Bender to drive the Shelby to Washington if I didn't participate in your sleazy little exhibition for Deke and the mechanics.'

Mal was obviously disconcerted by the reminder. A smear of red appeared on each of his high, slanting cheekbones. He averted his eyes, then cleared his throat.

'I was bluffing.'

He muttered it half under his breath, so that Abbie wasn't sure she'd heard right.

'What?'

He grimaced. 'I said I was bluffing.'

'I see,' she murmured.

'Are you going to pop your cork?' He looked and sounded as if he fully expected her to pop something . . . or someone.

Abbie pretended to give the question serious consideration. She should have been angry; downright furious, in fact. He had just admitted to using extortion to control and manipulate her. But, for some strange reason, seeing him like this—off balance, uncertain, slightly defensive—defused her anger. How could she rant and rave at him, when he looked like a little boy who'd been caught with his hand in the cookie jar?

'No, I'm not going to pop my cork.' She waited until his wary frown cleared, then added, 'Not now, anyway.'

The frown instantly reappeared. 'What does that mean?'

Abbie didn't answer until she'd scooted out of the car and dusted off the seat of her jeans. 'It means not now,' she said calmly. 'Here comes Deke. Looks like he bought something.'

'I sent him to get a radar detector,' Mal said as he closed the hatchback and removed the key from the lock. He was still frowning when he handed the key ring to Abbie. 'I detect a definite threat, here. Be warned, Abigail Prudence, I don't take kindly to being threatened. If you're going to throw a tantrum or something, let's just get it the hell over with.'

Abbie gave him a disdainful look. 'I assure you, Garrett, I don't throw tantrums. The radar detector was a good idea. I understand the newer models can pick up a radar signal from around a curve or over a hill.'

Mal planted his hands on his hips and squinted at her fiercely from beneath the bill of his cap. 'Let's stick to one subject, all right? Are you keeping score, is that it—mentally recording a little black mark next to my name every time I do or say something you don't like?'

Abbie smiled serenely. 'Something like that.'

His scowl deepened, but Deke arrived before he could voice whatever dark thoughts were lurking behind his hooded, brooding eyes. Sheriff Collier was only a couple of seconds behind Deke. Abbie returned the sheriff's greeting with a nervous smile and then used a quick trip to the ladies' room of Gladys's Café as an excuse to escape the amused gleam in the lawman's eyes. By the time she returned, the radar detector had been installed and it was time for the race to start.

CHAPTER NINE

'SPEED?'

Abbie checked the speedometer. 'Ninety-seven.' Mal's head snapped around, his eyebrows jammed together over his nose. 'Just kidding,' she said quickly. 'I'm still holding it at seventy, like you said.'

'Very funny,' he grumbled. He leaned over to check the odometer reading himself, then went back to his calculations. Abbie sighed softly, resigning herself to another stretch of tedious silence. Except for an occasional tense question such as the one he'd just asked, he'd hardly spoken during the hour they had been on the road.

She darted a curious look at the blue nylon sports bag resting between his feet. She'd first noticed the bag when Mal retrieved it from the back seat, just before Sheriff Collier started the race. She'd wanted to ask about it then, but there hadn't been time; the Sable's engine was already idling and both sides of the street were lined with excited spectators, most of them waving and yelling encouragement to Mal.

Abbie had felt the crowd's outpouring of support, their collective pride in one of their own, and her palms had suddenly gone cold and clammy. For the first time the enormity of the commitment she'd made, the responsibility she had thoughtlessly accepted, came home to her. These people were counting on her. They expected her to drive the Shelby to victory. To win the race. Not just for Mal, but for all of them. What in heaven's name had she got herself into? What business did she have pitting her puny skills against those of Tony Ferris, a world-class racing driver? She must be crazy.

Before her anxiety could escalate into a full-blown panic, Mal had signalled to Sheriff Collier that they were ready. Abbie watched, dry-mouthed and slightly nauseated, as the sheriff's right arm slowly rose from his side. For one crazy second she had considered switching off the engine and tendering her resignation. But, before thought could be translated to action, the green flag in Collier's hand had flashed down and her last chance to cut and run was gone.

As soon as they reached the open highway, the Sable had passed them in an impressive burst of speed. Abbie's right foot automatically applied more pressure to the accelerator. The Shelby leapt forward in response.

'Don't,' Mal said sharply. 'Let him go.'

'They must be doing eighty-five or ninety,' she had protested. 'If we don't at least keep up with them——'

'Don't worry,' he said calmly. 'They won't risk maintaining that speed for long. Tony's just showing off, trying to psych us out. Ease back to seventy and hold it there until I tell you to speed up. I want to make a few calculations between here and Joplin.'

Abbie had followed his instructions against her better judgement. Joplin, Missouri was a little over one hundred miles away, just across the state line. If she held their speed to seventy for the next hundred miles, they wouldn't have a prayer of catching the Sable. From the corner of her eye she saw Mal remove two items from the blue nylon bag. One of the objects was a pocket calculator; it took her a moment to identify the other as a slide rule.

'What are you doing . . . estimating our fuel consumption?'

She'd taken his soft grunt as an affirmative. He was

already absorbed in his calculations, and she prudently decided not to distract him with any more questions.

In a way, she had been glad that his attention was occupied. She'd been afraid he might follow up on that last exchange they'd had back in town, maybe demand to know how many black marks he had accumulated and for what. Abbie knew her own limits, and she'd just about reached them. She was wound as tight as the mainspring of a watch. She needed some time to calm down and recharge her emotional batteries before she engaged in another verbal sparring match.

The first long stretch of interstate highway was fairly straight and flat, which meant that driving didn't require a great deal of concentration. All she had to do was keep the tyres on the road and maintain a cruising speed of seventy miles per hour. It hadn't taken long for boredom to set in.

Some race, she thought glumly. The Sable had quickly become a distant white speck and eventually disappeared over the horizon. Tony and Roxanne were probably half-way to St Louis by now, and Mal just kept playing with his slide rule and his calculator.

'How are we doing?' she ventured to ask when they reached the toll booth on the Oklahoma side of the state line.

Mal spared her a brief, impatient glance. 'What?'

'I asked how we're doing. Fuel-wise, I mean. Are we OK, or should I keep my eye out for a service station?'

He heaved a put-upon sigh, then leaned over and tapped the fuel gauge directly in front of her. Abbie pressed her lips together and resisted the urge to leave behind five feet of rubber as she pulled away from the toll booth.

'I know what it says,' she told him. 'But the needle must be stuck. It hasn't budged since we started.'

'There's nothing wrong with the gauge,' he muttered as he went back to fiddling with his slide rule.

'There must be. I just told you, the needle hasn't moved since we——'

Mal gave up trying to concentrate on his figures and lifted his head to frown at her darkly. 'I checked all the instruments and the electrical system last night. Trust me, Abigail, the gauge is working perfectly. Now, will you kindly shut up so I can finish these calculations?'

Abbie mulled over what he'd said for the next eight miles. Either he was dead wrong and the gauge really was broken—which, she had to admit, didn't seem likely—or he had built an engine that practically ran on air. Every few seconds her eyes darted back to the needle, as if she thought she might catch it in the act of moving. Eventually she realised that it had in fact crept about a sixteenth of an inch to the right since they left the courthouse square. OK, so it wasn't stuck. Still, how many gallons of gasoline did sixteenth of an inch represent? One? Surely no more than that.

A growing excitement soon replaced her boredom. Mal had said that the winner would be the car that consumed the least amount of fuel and had the fewest mechanical problems during the trip. If the engine Roxanne had designed was as fuel-efficient as this one appeared to be…

By the time they reached the first Joplin exit, her always lively curiosity had become an intolerable itch. She could barely restrain the urge to start bombarding Mal with questions. Somehow she managed to wait until the second exit was behind them.

'We're passing Joplin now,' she announced, loudly enough to make sure she got his attention.

Mal looked up in surprise. 'Already?'

'We've been on the road more than an hour and a half. Have you finished your calculations?'

'For now.' He replaced the calculator and slide rule in the sports bag, then linked his fingers behind his head and arched his back to stretch out the kinks. Abbie allowed herself one quick peek at the way his shirt was pulled taut across his chest, then decided that, for safety's sake, she'd better keep her eyes on the road.

'Does that mean I can speed up?' she asked hopefully.

'I'd like to get there in one piece,' Mal drawled in reply.

'So would I. Preferably before noon Monday.'

'All right, you can take it up to eighty. But if the radar detector goes off——'

'I know, I know,' Abbie interrupted. 'I'll hit the brakes before the cops can lock on to us.' She waited until the speedometer registered eighty, then remarked casually, 'I figure we're getting between sixty and seventy miles to the gallon.'

Mal folded his arms over his chest and swivelled slightly to look at her. 'Oh, you figure that, do you?'

'I admit it's only a guesstimate. How close am I?'

'Close enough.' He shifted again, hooking his left arm over the seat back so that he was facing her. 'I won't have a precise figure until I can take a measurement of how much fuel we've used, but we should be averaging about sixty-seven miles per gallon.'

'Impressive,' Abbie said, and meant it. 'Those modifications you made must have been pretty radical.'

'Not really. Basically it amounted to replacing a few standard parts with components I designed to do the same jobs, only more efficiently. Any decent mechanic could have done it.'

Abbie heard the slight emphasis on 'any'. 'Hey, it was an honest mistake. You looked like you'd just finished the day shift at the corner Texaco station.'

'And you looked like you were just starting the night shift.'

A startled laugh escaped her. 'I beg your pardon!'

'Well, you were sashaying around a public bar in a see-through blouse and glow-in-the-dark eyelids.'

'You can't see through this blouse!' Abbie asserted, then cast a quick glance downwards to be sure. 'And I wasn't sashaying. I was just sitting there having a drink, minding my own business——'

'Eavesdropping,' Mal put in drily.

A sheepish smile tugged at her mouth. 'Well . . .'

'And when you heard me talking about the race, you came right over to solicit a job as my driver, bold as brass.'

'But I didn't do any sashaying,' she repeated firmly.

'You surely did,' he insisted.

'I wasn't coming on to you.' It seemed important that she make that clear, but she couldn't have said why.

'Did I say you were?'

'Well, it sounds like you thought I was.'

'Maybe not consciously,' he allowed in a hazily amused drawl.

Abbie opened her mouth, then abruptly closed it without making the retort that was on the tip of her tongue. It suddenly dawned on her that he was doing it again—changing the subject, deliberately distracting her so she wouldn't ask questions he didn't want to answer.

'I get the message, Garrett,' she said coolly.

'You do?' A note of puzzlement had joined the amusement in his voice.

'Loud and clear,' she assured him.

Mal cocked his head to one side, lips pursed, eyes narrowed. He studied her profile for several seconds, taking in her heightened colour and the contrary set of her jaw. 'Something tells me the message you got wasn't the one I thought I was sending,' he murmured. 'I wasn't putting you down.'

Abbie feigned enlightened surprise. 'Oh, I see. Ridiculing the way I dress and how much make-up I wear is your way of complimenting me. How typically perverse of you.'

'Dammit, I was only teasing.'

She shot him a withering look. 'Spare me, please. Anyway, it doesn't matter.'

'The hell it doesn't!' Mal snapped. His vehemence surprised Abbie, but she didn't let it show.

'It doesn't,' she reiterated. 'We both know you were only trying to sidetrack me . . . again. As I said, I got the message. I promise not to grill you about your precious top secret engine.'

She could feel him watching her in the pregnant silence that followed. 'And you call me perverse,' he muttered sourly. 'For your information, Abigail Prudence, you've jumped headfirst to the wrong conclusion . . . again.'

He sounded so perturbed that, if Abbie hadn't known better, she'd have thought she had said something to offend him. She favoured him with a sceptical glance.

'You don't believe me, do you?' he demanded.

She didn't, but she wasn't about to call him a liar to his face. She opted for a diplomatic retreat instead. 'Let's just forget it. I can understand why you're reluctant to tell me about the engine. You don't know much about me, after all. If I were the unscrupulous sort, I could probably——'

'What do you want to know?' he asked curtly.

'—sell whatever you told me to—— What?'

'Never mind, it would be simpler to just describe the modifications I made and the reasons for each of them.'

Which he proceeded to do. In detail. Abbie desperately tried to digest the avalanche of technical information, now and then interrupting with a succinct question or a request for clarification, and prayed that she would be able to remember one tenth of it when she sat down at the keyboard to write her story. Fortunately traffic was sparse, so she was able to devote most of her attention to what he was saying. Most of the other people traversing Missouri on I44 that afternoon were driving tractor-trailer rigs or moving vans, and most of them were travelling at least as fast as the Shelby.

By the time Mal finished answering the last of her questions, they had covered more than half the distance between Joplin and St Louis. He took out his calculator, checked the various gauges and announced that they were now averaging close to seventy miles per gallon.

'How can that be?' Abbie asked in confusion. Their present speed was ten miles an hour faster than when he had made the first set of calculations. The miles-per-gallon figure should be lower, not higher.

'I just explained how,' he said tersely. 'The object of the modifications I made was to increase fuel-efficiency. The faster we go, the less fuel the engine requires to do its job.'

There was an edge to his voice that Abbie hadn't heard for a while. He sounded irritable; almost surly, in fact. She turned her head to check out his expression. It matched his voice.

'Keep your eyes on the road, for God's sake,' he growled.

Abbie bit back a sarcastic reply. There was one eighteen-wheeler about half a mile ahead of them and two more—both in the left-hand lane—coming up fast from behind. It wasn't as if they were smack in the middle of rush-hour traffic.

'Are you sulking?'

She knew she sounded incredulous; she *was* incredulous. She felt the heat of Mal's glare even before she risked another glance at him and almost had her eyelashes singed off. He didn't deign to answer, tugging the bill of his cap low over his eyes and sliding down low in his seat.

'Let me rephrase that,' she murmured. '*Why* are you sulking?'

Just as she decided that that question was going to go unanswered, as well, he informed her coldly that 'mature adults do not sulk.'

'Mature adults don't wrap up a three-day binge by demolishing the neighbourhood bar, either,' Abbie informed him promptly.

As soon as she said it, she wished she hadn't. She waited for him to angrily ask how she knew about the episode at Ramey's Bar & Grill. But he surprised her.

'I guess one of the busybodies in town told you about that.' He sounded resentful, but not outraged.

'It's true, then?' she asked.

'Yes and no,' he muttered. 'I did make a mess of Ramey's place, but I gave him a blank cheque to cover the damages before I touched that first stick of furniture.'

Abbie couldn't resist. 'Very mature of you.'

'I thought so. I even waited for him to take down the mirrors and move most of the liquor to the back room. And, contrary to public opinion, I wasn't drunk,' he added indignantly. 'Hell, I'd only had a couple of beers. I just needed to let off some steam, and Ramsey's seemed like the natural place to do it.'

Abbie decided to postpone asking why he'd needed to let off steam. 'But if you paid Ramey ahead of time for the damages and he was willing to let you run amok in his bar, why did Sheriff Collier and two deputies come and take you to jail?'

Mal sent her a vexed look from beneath the bill of his cap. 'Did you also hear about the time I fell out of a tree when I was twelve and broke my arm in two places?'

Abbie hastily squelched a smile. 'No.'

'How about the time Mary Alice Henderson's dad discovered his daughter initiating me into the joys of sex behind his chicken coop?'

She suspected he was trying to shock and/or embarrass her into silence. 'I'm afraid that's another anecdote I missed. If you don't mind my asking, how old were you and Mary Alice at the time?'

'I was fourteen. She was almost eighteen.'

Abbie didn't bother to mask her surprise. 'Precocious little devil, weren't you?'

'Always,' he drawled. 'How old were you?'

She struggled with his meaning for a moment, then decided she'd better ask. 'How old was I the first time I——'

'Had sex.'

His voice was noticeably lower, and husky enough to make the fine hairs on her arms lift in reaction.

'That's a rather personal question, don't you think?'

'Extremely personal. How old?'

She considered refusing to answer. But, as Mal would no doubt point out, he had answered when she'd asked.

'Twenty-three.'

She was embarrassed and annoyed by the timid, almost apologetic way it came out. His reaction exacerbated her discomfort.

'Twenty-three!' His voice rang with stunned disbelief. 'You're putting me on.'

Abbie felt colour bloom in her cheeks. 'I assure you, I'm not.' Her cool, formal tone would have given any other man pause, made him back off. But not Mal. He sat up and pushed his cap back on his head.

'I don't get it. I thought you grew up on Army bases. Did your parents keep you locked in the attic or something?'

'Of course not,' she snapped. 'What a thing to say! I'll

have you know my parents are wonderful people.'

He leaned closer to peer at her. 'Well, it couldn't have been acne,' he murmured. 'Under all that war paint, your skin's as smooth as a baby's bottom.'

'Do you mind?' she protested hotly.

'Sorry,' he murmured as he subsided into his seat. 'I meant it as a compliment.'

But Abbie wasn't so easily mollified. 'You're carrying on as if I'm some kind of freak. So I was a virgin till I was twenty-three. Is that a crime?'

'I'm sure I'd have thought so,' he drawled, 'if I'd known you when you were twenty-two.'

Abbie thought it was a good thing she was driving. If her hands had been free, she might have wrapped them around his throat.

'I answered your question,' she said as calmly as she was able. 'Now, could we please change the subject?'

He tugged the bill of his cap back down to shield his eyes. 'I was just warming up to this subject.'

Abbie silently counted to ten, telling herself as she did that he was only needling her again, trying to make her lose her temper. Well, she wouldn't give him the satisfaction. She checked the mirrors, then smoothly changed lanes to pass a station wagon pulling a U-Haul trailer behind it.

'Do you really think it's wise to keep harassing me, when I'm driving your five-hundred-thousand-dollar car down an interstate highway at eighty miles per hour?'

Mal waited until they were back in the right-hand lane to remark, 'That's some chip you've got on your shoulder.'

'And what is that supposed to mean?' she demanded.

'Exactly what you think it means. You're determined to have your feathers ruffled, aren't you? Damned if you're not the most prickly, cantankerous female I've ever met.'

'Was that another compliment?' Abbie asked drily.

His husky chuckle was a surprise. 'Not to mention the most unpredictable. Truce?'

She shook her head. 'No, thanks. I've experienced your idea of a truce. I think I'd prefer all-out war . . . at least I'd know what to expect.'

He didn't respond to that. In fact, he was silent for so long that she decided he must have taken her at her word. One of the signs they passed informed her that they were forty-five miles from St Louis. Abbie wondered where and when Mal planned to stop, and whether she would have a chance to call Roger Zirkelbach when they did. Roger had probably worn a trench in the floor around his phone by now. Patience had never been his strong suit.

She was about to ask if he wanted her to stop before they reached St Louis or wait until they crossed the Mississippi into Illinois, when the small black box perched on the dash emitted a high-pitched beep. Abbie reacted instantly. Their speed had dropped to seventy by the time the second beep sounded.

Mal sat forward to scrutinise the traffic ahead. 'Do you see the police car?'

'No, but it must be close. A trucker in one of the westbound lanes just flashed his headlights. This may not be the ideal time to ask, but is Missouri one of the states that have outlawed radar detectors?'

'Damned if I know.' Just in case, Mal removed the box—which was now sending forth an irritating stream of *bee-bee-bee-bee-beeps*—from the dashboard and placed it on the floor. 'Are we legal?' he asked as he turned off the sound. A small red light continued to flash, signalling that the radar scan was still in effect.

'Barely. Assuming the speedometer is accurate.'

'It is,' he assured her. 'But the police equipment may

not be. Better drop down to sixty-three or four until we spot—— Sonofabitch! I don't believe it!'

His sudden exclamation alarmed Abbie. She instinctively reduced their speed even more. 'What? What is it?'

'Just ahead, on the other side of that overpass.' He laughed jubilantly and hit the dashboard with his fist. 'This is too good to be true. Slow down.'

Abbie opened her mouth to tell him they had already slowed to fifty-five, but then she saw what had caused his excitement. A smile spread over her face. A police cruiser was parked in the emergency lane, lights flashing. Just in front of the cruiser was another car. The driver was being ticketed, presumably for speeding. The second car was a white Sable; the man standing beside it, scowling furiously while he waited for the highway patrolman to finish writing the ticket, was Tony Ferris. Mal waved cheerfully as they passed.

'Did he see you?' Abbie asked as they left the Sable behind.

'Oh, yeah. He may get another ticket for making an obscene gesture in public.'

She grinned. 'He's probably wishing he'd stayed in Indianapolis. I thought they'd be a lot farther ahead of us by now. Maybe this isn't the first time they've been stopped for speeding.'

'Knowing Tony, I'd be surprised if it's only the second or third time,' Mal drawled. 'But I'm hoping the reason we caught up with them is because they made a pit stop somewhere.'

'To buy fuel, you mean?'

'Or to make an adjustment or, even better, a minor repair.' He replaced the radar detector on the dash and switched the sound back on. The box remained silent. 'OK, it should be safe to take it back up to eighty.'

'How about eighty-five?' Abbie suggested. 'At least till

we get to St Louis.'

'That's thirty miles per hour over the speed limit, Abigail.'

'So? Do you think Tony's going to stay under the legal limit, especially now that we've pulled ahead? I think we should increase our lead while we can.'

When Mal didn't reply, she glanced at him and discovered that he was watching her, his expression pensive.

'Is someting wrong?' she asked. 'You did say that the faster we go, the less fuel the engine requires to do its job. Shouldn't we be taking advantage of that fact?' Now that they had gained the lead, she didn't want to risk losing it again. She couldn't understand why Mal didn't seem to share her enthusiasm. It was his car, after all; his bet.

'You're really committed to winning, aren't you?'

The question didn't disconcert Abbie half as much as the surprise she heard in his voice.

'Isn't that the idea—to win?'

'Of course, but . . .' She had the feeling he was selecting his words with more care than usual. 'Now, don't get your feathers ruffled, but I didn't think it made much difference to you one way or the other who won, as long as you got to Washington by Monday.'

It was foolish of her, Abbie knew, but she was offended. No, she was hurt. *Idiot,* she admonished herself. What else was he supposed to think?

'I admit I felt that way in the beginning. And to be perfectly honest, when I saw Roxanne's car I didn't think we had a prayer of winning.' From the corner of her eye she saw Mal stiffen slightly. Terrific. Now his feathers were ruffled. She hastened to soothe them. 'But once I understood what an incredible job you've done redesigning the Shelby's engine, I guess my natural competitiveness took over.'

'Your natural competitiveness,' he repeated.

Abbie thought she detected a trace of scepticism in his voice. 'That's right,' she affirmed. 'I don't like to lose.' Which was the truest thing she'd said in the last twenty-four hours.

Mal regarded her thoughtfully. 'Go ahead and take it up to eighty-five.' Without pausing, he asked in the same matter-of-fact tone, 'Would you say you're a poor loser?'

'Always have been, probably always will be,' she admitted with a self-deprecating smile. 'When I was eliminated in the final round of the fifth grade spelling bee, I pouted for two days. Then I got mad—at myself, for not having studied harder. I made up my mind to win the next year.'

'And of course you did.'

'Of course. I told you last night, when I see something I want, I go after it. And what I want at the moment is for us to win this race and for you to win your bet.'

'Why?'

The question came at her from out of nowhere, catching her off guard. And though he'd spoken softly, she sensed that the answer was important to him. He confirmed the impression when he added just as softly, 'The truth, Abigail.'

She only hesitated for a moment. He wanted the truth, he deserved the truth, and the truth was what she would give him, at least this once. She didn't have to search for it; it was within easy reach, waiting to be recognised and accepted. And, ironically, it had nothing to do with an exclusive once-in-a-lifetime feature article about Malachi Garrett and/or fuel-efficient engines.

'I want us to win because I can't stand the thought of your falling into Roxanne Winston's clutches.'

She risked a quick glance at him, anticipating that his ruggedly handsome face would be sporting a smug, purely masculine smirk. He was smiling, but it was a warm, disturbingly intimate smile. Abbie quickly looked away. She tried to swallow and discovered that her mouth was too dry.

'I like a woman who doesn't mince words,' he said in the sexy murmur that never failed to arouse her.

'Don't get any ideas, Garrett,' she warned. 'We have an agreement, remember.'

His soft, husky laugh sent ripples of sexual awareness all the way to her toes. 'You sound a little nervous, Abigail. Are you afraid I won't honour the agreement . . . or that I will?'

The relaxed, teasing humour in his voice eased Abbie's tension somewhat. 'Do you honestly expect me to answer that question?'

A second's pause preceded his reply. 'Darlin', if there's one thing I've learned about you, it's to expect the unexpected. Just keep in mind that what's sauce for goose . . .'

Abbie didn't respond to the cautionary advice. She was too busy trying to cope with her spontaneous, distressingly powerful reaction to that huskily drawled 'Darlin' '.

CHAPTER TEN

THEY stopped at a service station in Webster Groves, just south-west of St Louis. Mal immediately removed a tool-box from the rear of the Shelby and took out a thin telescoping tube, which he proceeded to poke into the fuel tank. Abbie stood to one side and watched for a minute or so.

'Is there anything I can do to help?'

He answered without looking up. 'No—thanks, anyway. I'm just going to make a few checks, then we'll get something to eat at that restaurant next door.'

'OK,' she murmured. A casual survey of the area turned up no less than three pay phones. 'If you're sure you don't need me, I think I'll make a quick phone call while I'm waiting.'

Mal did look up then. His mouth tilted in a brief, enigmatic smile before he returned his attention to his work. 'Give Larry my regards.'

Abbie stared at him blankly. 'Larry?'

'Your boyfriend,' he reminded her. 'The one who left you high and dry. Surely you haven't forgotten him already?'

'Oh, *that* Larry.' Amazingly, her voice sounded relatively normal. 'No. I mean, that's not who I want to call. I thought I'd better get in touch with the doctor I'm supposed to start working for and let him know I'm on the way.'

She didn't give him a chance to reply, hurrying off toward the nearest phone before he could think of any questions to ask her about the doctor. She took a chance and called the *Post*. Fortunately, Roger was still at his desk.

'Abbie, thank God! Where are you? Is the race still on? Please tell me it's still on!'

'It's still on,' Abbie said obligingly. 'We're a few miles west of St Louis. Roger, is something wrong? You sound even more hyper than usual.'

His exuberant laugh came through clearly. 'Nothing's wrong. Just the opposite, in fact. After I talked to you yesterday, I remembered that next week the House starts another round of hearings on alternative fuels and fuel-efficient engines.'

A chill of premonition slithered down Abbie's spine. 'What?' she said faintly.

Evidently Roger hadn't heard her. He kept talking enthusiastically. 'I don't know why I didn't remember when you first mentioned the race. You did say both cars are equipped with experimental engines?'

'Yes,' Abbie murmured. 'Experimental fuel-efficient engines. This is the first road test for both of them.'

'Better and better!' Roger gloated. 'The timing couldn't have been more perfect if the race had been planned to coincide with the hearings.'

Abbie sagged against the phone. She felt slightly ill. 'I think it was.' She filled him in quickly, explaining that Roxanne Winston had designed the other car's engine and how Roxanne had leaked information about the race to an editor in Washington.

'But Garrett was adamantly anti-publicity,' she added. 'He was ready to call the whole thing off, until Roxanne phoned the editor and told him the race has been cancelled.'

'Oh, boy,' Roger muttered. 'So where does that leave you?'

'Between the frying pan and the fire,' Abbie replied

glumly. 'He's going to assume I knew about the hearings all along. He'll probably figure I came to Oklahoma for the sole purpose of checking out his precious engine. He may even think that somehow I managed to find out about the race, and that was why I came. He'll kill me,' she concluded with grim certainty.

'Don't even think about scrapping this story, Abbie,' Roger warned. 'You made a commitment, and I intend to hold you to it. It would be unprofessional as hell for you to back out now. If word got around——'

'Don't threaten me, Roger,' she interrupted coldly. 'I'll deliver the damned story, don't worry.'

Reassured, he immediately back-pedalled, going so far as to offer reimbursement for any emergency medical expenses she might incur in the line of duty. Abbie wasn't amused. When he pressed her to check in with him as often as possible, she said she would try and then deliberately hung up on him.

'You'll try what?'

She spun around, one hand pressed to her chest. 'You must be part Indian,' she said to Mal, who was standing behind her, wiping his hands on an old T-shirt.

He grinned. 'I wouldn't be a bit surprised. Did you get hold of the doctor?'

'Uh . . . no. He was out of the office . . . at the hospital. His receptionist took my message, but I said I'd try to call again later, just in case he doesn't receive it. Have you finished checking the car? Can we eat now?'

'Hungry, are you?' Mal drawled. He slung the grease-stained shirt over his shoulder and clasped her hand to lead her towards the restuarant. 'I told you to fill up at breakfast.'

Abbie knew it was a mistake to link her fingers with his, but she did it anyway. Half-way across the restaurant car park she realised that he'd shortened his normally long,

loping stride, taking smaller steps so she wouldn't have to
trot to keep up with him. So he could be considerate, as
well as funny and charming and devastatingly seductive.
She heaved a dejected sigh. Darn the man for getting
under her skin. Darn her for letting him. It would have
been hard enough to face his scorn and contempt when
he discovered that she'd deliberately deceived him,
without the added misery of knowing she was more than
half-way to falling in love with him.

Half an hour later they were back on the interstate,
heading into St Louis. The roast beef sandwich Abbie
had wolfed down sat like a rock in her stomach. She
suspected that the antacid tablets Irma had given her were
going to come in handy before long.

'I don't understand why we had to eat so fast,' she
complained as they passed a van with frolicking unicorns
painted on the side. 'Would it have hurt to spend an hour
enjoying a nice, leisurely dinner?'

'We can be half-way across Illinois in an hour,' Mal
replied. 'I thought you wanted to win this race.'

'I do. It's just that normally I like to chew my food
before I swallow it.'

The sarcastic remark earned her a good-natured
chuckle, which merely surprised her, and a light tap on
the chin, which startled her so badly that she almost
swerved the Shelby into an oil tanker in the next lane.

'Garrett!' she croaked when her heart had vacated her
throat.

'Sorry,' he murmured. 'I didn't realise you were so
goosey. I won't do it again.'

'See that you don't!'

'At least, not while you're driving,' he added mildly.

Abbie turned her head to give him a suspicious look and
found him grinning wickedly. 'Now, listen, Garrett——'

She abruptly cut herself off when she saw a diamond-shaped orange sign flash past his window. 'What did that sign say?'

'What sign?'

'The one we just passed.'

Mal shrugged. 'I didn't see it. I was watching your ears for signs of steam. It was probably one of those information things—take two-seventy north to the airport, or something like that. We've passed a dozen of them.'

Abbie shook her head. 'No. This sign wasn't green and it wasn't rectangular. It was an orange diamond—the kind they put up when a section of road is under construction or there's a detour ahead. You'd better get out the atlas.'

Twenty minutes later Mal was hunched over the road atlas, which was lying open on his lap, scowling as he tried to decipher the maze of intersecting, numbered lines.

'Well?' Abbie said impatiently. 'Have you figured out where we are?'

'I'm not sure. I think we should have gone north instead of south at that first detour.'

'That was eleven or twelve miles back, for pity's sake. Why didn't you say something right away?'

'Obviously because I didn't realise we were going in the wrong direction right away,' he said snidely.

'You told me to go south,' Abbie reminded him.

'Well, I was wrong,' he growled. 'I made a mistake. So sue me.'

She drew a deep, calming breath. This was getting them nowhere. 'I apologise for snapping at you. I guess fighting all this traffic has got me a little tense. I've never seen so many trucks and buses in my life.'

Mal cleared his throat softly. 'I think that's because we took the truck route at the second detour.'

'What?'

'Well, it was either that or end up in Memphis!

According to the damned signs, those were the only two choices we had.'

'Wrong, Einstein. We could have stopped and asked somebody for directions.'

Better late than never, she thought as she took advantage of a red light to look around for a likely source of help. They were in luck. She spotted a fire station on the cross street, only half a block away, and parked near it.

'Why are you stopping here?' Mal asked with a frown.

Abbie answered as she unbuckled her seat-belt and opened her door. 'Because firemen usually know their way around a city better than anybody, including the cops. They also have to know all the shortcuts. Bring the atlas.'

The fire fighters were friendly and eager to be of assistance, especially when they got a look at the Shelby. It turned out that two of them were members of a sports car club and had been trying to find one to race at a local track.

'I bet she'll really fly,' the younger of the two said enviously when directions had been given and Mal and Abbie were ready to leave. 'What's her top speed?'

The question was directed at Mal. Without missing a beat he drawled, 'I wouldn't know. I'm just the mechanic.'

Abbie quickly climbed behind the wheel and started the engine before the young man could ask *her* anything about the car.

The directions the firemen had given them took them through downtown St Louis, around Busch Stadium and eventually on to I55 East. Abbie sighed in relief as they passed the Gateway Arch and started across the Mississippi, but she didn't completely relax until they passed a sign indicating that they were on I64, two hundred and fifty miles from Louisville, Kentucky, and she knew they were headed in the right direction.

'Hallelujah,' Mal said drily. 'I'd started to think I was going to spend my next birthday in St Louis.'

Abbie didn't reply. She was still annoyed with him for getting them lost and costing them precious time.

'It was a smart move to stop at a fire station,' he said after a moment. 'I never would have thought of it.'

'I can believe that,' she muttered under her breath.

'There's no need to be sarcastic.'

'Sorry,' Abbie said. She didn't even try to sound sincere.

She heard his gusty sigh. 'We only lost about forty-five minutes. We can make it up between here and Louisville.'

Her temper flared at the irritation in his voice. What right did *he* have to be irritated? It was his fault they had gone off course and wasted three quarters of an hour.

'Right,' she said flatly. 'We can make up a measly forty-five minutes, no trouble. I just wish we'd spent the time having dinner, instead of following a truck convoy all over St Louis.'

'All right,' Mal muttered. 'You've made your point.'

' "We can be half-way across Illinois in an hour," ' she quoted, mimicking his drawl.

'All *right*, dammit! I screwed up. Is that what you want to hear?'

'It'll do,' she said. 'For starters.'

'God, you're a shrew.'

Two angry splotches appeared on Abbie's cheeks. 'In that case, maybe you'd like to trade places with Tony . . . provided we ever catch up with him again.'

'That was a typically asinine, typically *female* remark,' Mal said in disgust. 'The only thing worse than being stuck with you for the next thousand miles would be being stuck with Roxie.'

Abbie feigned amazement. 'You mean she's an even

bigger shrew than I am?'

'Honey, she makes you look like Mother Teresa.'

It was Abbie's turn to be snide. 'Evidently you didn't always feel that way.'

'Oh, I always suspected she had the potential to be a first-class bitch. I was just too far gone to care.'

Abbie tried to identify the emotion in his voice. Was it self-mockery, or bitterness?

'That doesn't sound like you.' She was careful to keep her tone neutral. She wanted him to keep talking about his relationship with Roxanne; not for the sake of any story, but for herself, to satisfy her own morbid curiosity.

'Ain't it the truth,' he drawled. 'I guess everybody's entitled to make a fool of himself once in his life. But I learned my lesson. Never again.'

Abbie had a feeling she would regret asking, but she didn't seem able to help herself. 'What was the lesson?'

'That any man who puts his faith in a woman's integrity gets exactly what he deserves. You're all the same—always looking out for number one, using anybody stupid enough to let himself be used, taking whatever you can get . . . usually from some poor slob who doesn't have sense enough to realise he's been taken for the ride of his life.'

Abbie didn't respond to his little speech until she had examined her own reaction to it and decided she wasn't just being defensive.

'I've heard a lot of chauvinistic garbage in my life, Garrett, but what just came out of your mouth sets a new standard,' she said with far more calm than she felt.

'I can see this is going to be a delightful evening,' he growled in response. 'You asked what lesson I learned, and I told you. If you didn't want to hear the answer, you shouldn't have asked the question.'

'You don't honestly believe all that crap,' Abbie said with conviction. 'You're too intelligent to make such idiotic, irresponsible generalisations.'

'Thanks,' he muttered. 'I think.'

'Just because one woman took advantage of you—how many years ago?'

'Almost three. And she didn't just "take advantage" of me. She set me up, used me, then gave me the old heave-ho when she'd got what she was after. Namely the plans for the artificial heart I was working on at the time. She took them to a talented but naïve young doctor and convinced him he'd be doing a great service for mankind if he finished refining the design. The guy was a brilliant heart surgeon, but unfortunately he didn't know diddly about biomedical engineering.'

Abbie was stunned. No wonder he had such a low opinion of women. Apparently he'd never known one who hadn't put her own selfish interests first.

'All right,' she murmured. 'I'll grant that what Roxanne did was terrible.'

'Gee, that's big of you.'

She ignored the sarcastic comment. 'But you must realise how irrational it is to let that one rotten experience prejudice you against every woman you meet.'

'I never claimed to be rational, Abigail,' he drawled. 'Just extremely cautious.'

'Distrustful,' she corrected.

'OK, distrustful,' he admitted grudgingly. 'But with good reason.'

Abbie noticed that the sky had darkened to dusk. She reached down to switch on the headlights, then spared a moment to check the gauges.

'Have you let any woman get close to you since Roxanne left?'

There was no humour in Mal's harsh bark of laughter. 'Hell, no! I'm chauvinist, remember, not a masochist.'

Abbie privately thought that what he was was a man

who had been hurt once and wasn't about to risk letting it happen again. 'Tell me about her,' she asked quietly.

'Who, her? Roxanne?' He sounded incredulous.

'Yes, Roxanne.'

He shifted restlessly. 'I don't want to talk about her.'

'You should, you know,' Abbie murmured in the same quiet, non-threatening voice. 'You've kept all your resentment and bitterness about the way she betrayed you locked up inside for almost three years, and it's been festering all that time . . . poisoning you.'

'God,' he muttered. 'You make me sound like a walking, talking boil.'

'You know I'm right,' she insisted. 'Where did you meet her?'

'I said I don't want to talk about her! And what difference does it make where I met her, for pity's sake?'

Abbie shrugged. 'It seemes like the logical place to start.'

By the time they reached Mt Vernon, Illinois, she'd learned that Roxanne had been one of the students in an advanced engineering course he had taken over for an ailing faculty member one spring at Purdue University. That revelation had been quite a shock; Abbie had trouble imagining him in the role of professor. She wondered if he'd presented his lectures in a grease-stained sweatshirt and jeans.

Roxanne had been the brightest and most ambitious of his students. Equally important, she had been totally unlike the endless succession of women who paraded in and out of his father's life. She was intelligent, independent, and aggressively goal-orientated. Mal had fallen hard and fast. A week after receiving a Master's in electrical engineering, Roxanne returned with him to Oklahoma. She stayed for almost two years.

'Those last few months, I knew she'd started to feel

restless,' he admitted. 'After she left I realised she'd been sending out warning signals for some time. I guess I just didn't want to acknowledge them.' He paused, sighing heavily.

'Hell, I couldn't really blame her for leaving. I'm not the easiest person in the world to live with. When I get deeply involved in a project, nothing and no one else exists. Sometimes I forget to eat or sleep for days at a time, and I'm lousy company. What I'll never forgive is the cold-blooded way she set me up and used me.'

'Have you ever considered that she may not have thought of it that way?' Abbie murmured. She could hardly believe she was playing devil's advocate for Roxanne Winston, but, in all fairness, she felt he should at least consider the possibility that Roxanne hadn't 'set him up', as he'd assumed. 'Had she been helping you with your work, specifically with the artificial heart?'

'I know what you're getting at, Abigail, but you're way off base,' Mal replied. 'Yes, she'd been assisting me, but it was *my* project, my design. There was never any question about that. She took the plans, then passed them off as her own work to get financing from some big-shot money man on Wall Street. Within a week she'd moved in with Mr Moneybags, set herself up with an office and a staff, and started contacting potential clients . . . including several people she'd met while she was working with me. Every move was calculated, believe me. Roxanne doesn't have an impulsive bone in her body. She knew exactly what she was doing from the very beginning.'

Abbie experienced a sudden flash of insight. 'That's what galls you most, isn't it—the idea that she was plotting to use you all along, and you never suspected a thing?'

'Of course it is,' he said irritably. 'No man likes to admit he let a woman make an utter fool of him, though lord knows it happens to all of us, sooner or later.'

'If that's true, it doesn't say much for the intelligence of the average man, does it?' Abbie murmured.

'I think it says more about the treacherous nature of the average woman,' he countered.

'Of course, you would. She zapped you right in the old ego, didn't she?'

She knew she'd hit the mark, even before his indignant retort. 'I don't believe you! First you nag me into spilling my guts——'

'I didn't nag,' Abbie said firmly. 'I encouraged you to talk, that's all.'

Mal blithely ignored the distinction. 'And *then*, when I've told you all the intimate details of an extremely traumatic experience, all you can say is "she zapped you right in the old ego". The depth of your sensitivity astounds me.'

'Be honest, Garrett,' Abbie said drily. 'Which did Roxanne do more damage to—your heart, or your pride?'

He didn't answer right away. She waited patiently. 'Are you writing a book?' he finally muttered. He couldn't possibly have crammed any more sarcasm into six syllables.

'No, just curious. Well? Are you going to answer my question?'

'You have got to be the most stubborn, disagreeable, aggravating—not to mention nosy—female I've ever met,' Mal complained, but his relaxed drawl let Abbie know that he didn't mean a word of it.

'You forgot pain in the ass,' she said with a grin, and was rewarded with a husky chuckle. 'I guess you're not going to answer the question.'

'You already know the answer,' he told her drily. 'It was my pride that suffered the most serious damage.' He waited a moment, then added softly, 'You were right. I did need to talk about it. Thanks.'

'Don't mention it,' Abbie murmured. She didn't add

anything more. For some reason, that quiet, sincere 'thanks' had caused her eyes to mist over and a lump to form in her throat.

While she was relieved to know he wasn't carrying a torch for Roxanne, that fact didn't lessen her anxiety about her own situation. She had used him, too. Not as ruthlessly, perhaps, but she *was* furthering her own career at his expense.

If she could have seen a way out of the complicated mess she had created, she would have taken it. But Roger had made it clear that, as far as he was concerned, they had a verbal contract. If she didn't deliver the article she'd promised him, she had no doubt that he would do everything he could to see that she never sold another story to a major newspaper.

Would Mal ever forgive her? Would he even give her a chance to explain? She considered telling him everything now, rather than waiting until they arrived in Washington. But if she did, she suspected he might be so furious that he would order her to stop the car and get out, or at the very least dump her at the next exit. Then what would happen? Even if he continued on without her, he wouldn't have a chance of winning the race. The man might be a genius when it came to building automobile engines and artificial hearts, but he couldn't read a map to save his life. He'd probably end up lost somewhere in Appalachia, if he managed to get that far.

No, she realised with something like despair, she couldn't tell him until the race was over. Hopefully they would win, and he would be so elated that he wouldn't actually strangle her on the steps of the Capitol Building. She refused to speculate about what he *would* do, or what expression she would see in his eyes when he discovered her deceit.

Mal had taken the pocket calculator out of the sports

bag and placed it on the dash, next to the radar detector. Every few miles he picked it up, punched out a series of numbers, then replaced it on the dash.'

'Are you keeping track of our mileage?' Abbie asked as they approached the Illinois-Indiana border.

'Yes. I figure we've consumed almost eight gallons of fuel so far. The gauge should show about three-eighths of a tank left, maybe a little more than that.'

Abbie checked. 'Right on the nose. How much farther do you want to go before we stop to fill up?'

He thought for a moment. 'We should be able to make it to Louisville.'

'Louisville!' she repeated in surprise. 'That's got to be at least another hundred miles.'

'More like a hundred and twenty. But we've got at least four gallons left in the tank. We're in good shape.'

'Speak for yourself, Ace. You and the car may be in good shape, but my neck is stiff, my back and shoulders ache, I'm getting pins and needles in my right leg and my bottom is starting to go numb.'

'Well, why didn't you say something sooner, for Pete's sake?' he muttered with a combination of exasperation and gruff concern that went a long way toward alleviating Abbie's aches and pains.

'I thought—I *hoped*—we'd be stopping before long. We must have come five hundred miles already.'

'Approximately five hundred and twenty,' Mal said softly. As he spoke, his left hand crept across her shoulder and began to gently knead the back of her neck.

Abbie instantly tensed. 'What are you——?'

'Just loosening you up a bit,' he murmured. 'Sorry, love. I should have realised you'd be stiff after so many hours at the wheel. Is that helping?'

Helping? He had to be kidding. If either his touch or his voice got any more sensual, she wasn't sure she'd be able to keep the car on the road. Holding her head up already required a conscious effort—it wanted to loll back and settle into his palm. And as for her hands . . . She locked her fingers around the steering wheel and refused to dwell on what they would prefer to be doing.

'Um, Garrett . . .' She cleared her throat, hoping to rid her voice of its telltale huskiness.

'Yes, love?'

Abbie's breathing faltered for a moment between inhale and exhale. Not only had he called her 'love' for the second time in as many minutes, suddenly his mouth was right next to her ear.

'I think you'd better stop that.'

His lips brushed her earlobe, his breath hot and moist. His fingers slipped into her hair. She was aware of the exact instant his touch changed, became a caress.

'You do?' His breathy, teasing whisper seemed to penetrate her skin and shiver down her spine.

'I do,' she gasped. 'Unless you wouldn't mind having your five-hundred-thousand-dollar car wrapped around a telephone pole.'

'There aren't any telephone poles along the interstate,' he murmured. A second later the tip of his tongue entered her ear.

Abbie's startled jerk didn't affect her steering, but the knowledge that it could have sent a bolt of panic ripping through her.

'*Garrett!*'

'Take it easy,' he soothed as he settled back in his seat. 'Don't blow a gasket. I'll behave from now on. Cross my heart.'

'And hope to die?' she asked shrilly. 'Are you suicidal, is that it? Do you have a death wish or something?'

'Of course not,' he scoffed. 'Calm down, Abigail.'

'Don't tell me to "calm down" in that damned patronising tone, you . . . jerk!'

Mal rushed to defend himself. 'I wasn't being patronising! I just——'

'Why don't *you* drive for a while? I'll run my fingers through *your* hair and poke my tongue in *your* ear while we're cruising along at eighty miles per hour, and we'll see how *calmly* you react.'

'Maybe you'd better pull over,' he suggested. 'At least until you get a grip on yourself.'

'If I stop this car,' Abbie told him flatly, 'you'll drive it the rest of the way to Louisville. Unless you're willing to do that, you'd better just shut up and leave me alone until we get there. And keep your hands and your tongue and every other part of you on your own side of the car!'

She didn't have to be told that she'd over-reacted. She was well aware of that fact. She was also aware that Mal had no idea what to make of her. He didn't say a word for the next hour and a half, though every now and then she felt the touch of his uneasy, slightly wary gaze. If her emotions hadn't been in such a state of upheaval, she might have seen the humour in the situation. She doubted that Malachi Garrett had ever been intimidated by a woman in his life, until now.

They were only a few miles from Louisville when Abbie remembered the complicated snarl of interchanges that had aptly been dubbed Spaghetti Junction by area residents. A couple of years ago she and some friends had driven down for the Kentucky Derby. Somehow they'd misinterpreted the directions on one of the signs and got into the wrong lane of traffic. Someone had realised their mistake almost at once, but they were across the Ohio River, heading for Indianapolis, before they found a place to turn around. She had no desire to repeat that experience. At least, not tonight, when she was physically and mentally exhausted, emotionally drained, and her nerves could have been used to string a banjo.

Among the increasing number of billboards the Shelby's headlights swept across was one advertising a Holiday Inn at the next exit. She considered asking Mal if it would be all right to stop there for the night, then decided not to bother. She needed to soak her cramped, aching muscles in a tub of hot water; to scrub off the make-up clogging her pores; to sit down in a decent restaurant and savour a meal that hadn't been reheated in a microwave oven. She was *going* to stop, and if he didn't like it he could take the car and finish the trip by himself.

'There's a Holiday Inn at the next exit,' he said out of the blue. 'Why don't we stop there for the night?'

Abbie's lips quirked in a wry smile. 'Whatever you say,' she murmured as she activated the right turn signal.

She hobbled around the car park, trying to work the kinks out of her joints, while Mal went into the office to secure two rooms.

'There's only one room available,' he said when he returned. 'But it has two double beds. Do you want to take it?'

Abbie noticed that he kept the Shelby between them when he told her. She gave him a hard, suspicious look over the roof.

'If you don't believe me, you can go inside and ask the manager yourself,' he said curtly. 'I'm not any happier about it than you are. Considering the mood you're in, I'd sooner share a room with Godzilla.'

'Tell him we'll take it,' she snapped.

'Fine!' he snapped back, then spun on his heel and stalked back inside.

When they drove around the building to park the Shelby outside their room, they discovered a white Sable occupying the space in front of the room next door.

CHAPTER ELEVEN

ABBIE switched off the engine and turned to Mal. 'It's them, isn't it?'

He nodded grimly. 'It's them.'

'Are you thinking what I'm thinking?'

'I don't know. Are you thinking we should let the air out of their tyres?'

'No, I'm thinking that if we can get back on the road before they realise we're here, we could be so far ahead of them by morning that they'd never catch up.'

His mouth started to curve in an appreciative smile, but then suddenly he sobered, shaking his head. 'You've been driving for more than nine hours. You need some rest.'

Abbie was touched by his thoughtfulness, and she knew he was right. Still, she hated to pass up this opportunity to regain the lead. 'All I really need is a hot bath and a hot meal, in that order, and I'll be ready to to again.'

Mal reached over and removed the key from the ignition. 'I think we'd better add a couple of hours' sleep to that list,' he said as he opened his door. 'Otherwise you'd be a hazard to everybody on the highway.'

He collected the blue nylon bag, her suitcase and a duffel bag he'd packed for himself, and carried them into the room. Abbie followed, intending to convince him that they should get back on the road as soon as possible. A tidal wave of deliciously cool air greeted her at the door. Her resolve wavered. Then she saw the two large, sinfully comfortable-looking beds.

'Now that you mention it, I guess I could use a short nap.'

Mal deposited their luggage on the floor of the small wardrobe and turned around in time to see her collapse face down on the bed nearest the door. 'I think I've died and gone to heaven,' she muttered into the quilted peach spread.

She felt the mattress sag, and then the brush of his lips against her nape. 'Poor baby,' he murmured. Before Abbie could decide how to react, he sat up and began to gently massage the tension from her aching shoulders.

'I'm sorry I called you a shrew,' he said as his hands slowly worked their way down her back. The silk blouse shifted beneath his long, supple fingers, sliding sensuously against her skin. Abbie closed her eyes and promised herself she would remind him about their hands-off agreement in just a minute or two . . . or five, or twenty. His hands reached her waist, tugged gently at the blouse, and suddenly there was no silk barrier between his skin and hers.

'What are you doing?' she asked drowsily, as if she didn't know perfectly well that he was preparing to undress her.

Mal slid one lean hand under her stomach, calm as you please, and unsnapped her jeans. 'You can't take a bath with your clothes on.'

He had a point there. And as long as he was only trying to be helpful . . .

'You're a very considerate man,' she mumbled, the words sort of slurring together. 'For a chauvinist pig.'

The mattress rocked, then tilted, alerting her that he was no longer just sitting on the edge. A second later his breath fanned the back of her neck. 'Roll over, and I'll show you how considerate I can be.'

Abbie shook her head. 'Uh-uh.' She might be dog-tired and half asleep, but thankfully her instinct for self-preservation still seemed to be functioning.

Mal's left hand crept under the tail of her blouse and started inching up her side. 'Scared?' he taunted softly.

Abbie didn't even consider lying. 'Yes.'

His index finger lazily stroked the outer curve of her breast. 'Of me?'

'Yes. No.' She inhaled sharply, trying to jolt her torpid brain out of its stupor. 'Of you, and me . . . us.' His finger strayed to her nipple. 'Oh, God. Mal, you prom——'

Her throat closed, choking off the rest of the reminder. Both his hands were suddenly inside her blouse, forming warm cradles for her breasts. Even more shocking was the unexpected weight of his body as he eased himself over to lie full-length on top of her.

'Am I too heavy?' he murmured in her ear.

'Yes!' Abbie gasped. Her hands scrabbled across the bedspread, frantically seeking something to anchor themselves to.'

'Liar.' The growled accusation vibrated through her as he dragged his open mouth up the side of her neck to her ear. His teeth nipped lightly at the lobe. His tongue apologised for the love-bite, then lingered to make reparation. And all the while his nimble fingers were doing the most incredible things to her breasts, making them throb with a pleasure so acute it was almost pain. As if the torment he was already inflicting wasn't enough, he deliberately tilted his pelvis into the curve of her bottom.

'Feel that?'

Abbie nodded once, not trusting her voice. She felt ready to burst into flames, and resisting the urge to move against him required every ounce of will-power she possessed. Her fingers tortured the bedspread.

'I've been in this sorry condition most of the day,' Mal

said roughly. 'My hands have been itching to touch you for the last three hundred miles. I've damn near worn out that stupid calculator just to give them something to do, to keep them from reaching for you.' He paused to draw a deep, ragged breath. 'That's why, when you said your neck was stiff—— All I intended to do was give you a little massage, I swear. But once I'd touched you, I just . . . got carried away.'

Abbie understood completely. If her own hands ever released their desperate grip on the bedspread, she would be in serious danger of getting carried away herself.

'Lord, I want you.' He breathed it into her ear, so softly that she wasn't certain he'd actually spoken the words aloud; with such aching need that the last trace of her reserve evaporated.

'I know,' she whispered. 'I want you, too.'

Mal's chest expanded, pressing against her back, then retreated as he expelled a long, sighing breath. 'That's good to know,' he said in the warm, honey-smooth drawl that never failed to stir her senses. 'For a while there I thought I'd made your Ten Most Detestable Chauvinists list.'

Abbie smiled. 'For a while there, you occupied the number one spot,' she told him candidly. 'But I still wanted you, even when I was busy detesting you for being such a chauvinist swine.'

He pressed his cheek to her hair and his arms contracted in a brief, hard hug. A sound that was half-laugh, half-groan broke from his throat. 'Mercy, Abigail! You make it damned hard for a man to behave himself.'

'You call this behaving yourself?' she scoffed. 'Luring me into a motel room with the promise of a hot bath and some much-needed rest, then climbing on top of me and taking all kinds of liberties, when you know I'm too exhausted to fight you off?'

His throaty laugh was so sexy, it should have been rated X. 'Believe me, darlin', considering the liberties I'd like to take——' he rocked his hips slowly, just in case she didn't understand his meaning '—I'm showing remarkable restraint.'

Which was an understatement if Abbie had ever heard one. 'You're not going to make love to me, are you?' she asked softly.

'I certainly am,' he murmured, nuzzling her ear. 'But not tonight.'

'Why not?'

'Because I don't want it to be just a quick tumble. I want us to have all night, maybe all the next day, too. I also want you to be an active participant, not just a spectator.'

'In other words,' Abbie concluded wryly, 'I should be wide awake and capable of fighting you off.'

He laid a feather-like kiss on her temple. 'You won't, though.'

'No,' she agreed with another small smile.

'It'll be good, for both of us.'

The whispered promise sent anticipatory shivers all the way to Abbie's toes. Her hands released the bedspread and reached back, finding the taut mounds of his buttocks. 'Yes,' she said with husky certainty. 'Better than good.'

Mal allowed her hands to remain where they were until they started to stroke, and then he abruptly pulled his from beneath her and rolled away with a muffled groan.

'Stay right there,' he ordered as he climbed off the bed. 'Don't get up for at least fifteen minutes.'

Abbie lifted her head and glanced over her shoulder. 'Why not? I'm dying for a long, hot bath.'

'At the risk of being called a selfish macho beast or worse, I think my need for a cold shower is greater than your need for a hot bath.'

She rolled to her side, propping herself up on an elbow. 'Mmm.'

He scowled at her. 'If you don't stop looking at me like that, you may never get your bath.'

Before she could come up with a saucy reply, he had snatched his duffel bag out of the wardrobe and disappeared into the bathroom. There was a distinct *click* as he locked the door. Abbie fell back against the pillows, her eyes closed and her arms wrapped around her midriff. The warm glow of happiness inside her couldn't last, she knew, but she intended to hang on to it for as long as she could.

Mal emerged from the bathroom fourteen minutes later wearing a clean pair of jeans and nothing else. Abbie allowed herself one sweeping glance that took in his gleaming, slicked-back hair and glorious, temptingly bare chest before she ducked past him.

'Don't lock it,' he said as she started to close the door.

'Why not?' she demanded. 'You did.'

'True, but it's damn near impossible to fall asleep and drown in an ice-cold shower,' he told her drily.

Abbie left the door unlocked. She had just gingerly climbed into the tub, which was filled to the overflow drain with steaming water, when Mal opened the door and slipped into the bathroom. He was perched on the tub's rim, one hand clamped over her mouth, before she could do more than emit a startled squawk and cross her arms over her breasts.

'Shh, don't kick up a ruckus,' he whispered urgently. 'We've been discovered. Tony's here.'

Abbie left one arm to guard her breasts and reached up to yank his hand away. 'Here? You mean *here*—in our room?'

Mal nodded. His fingers absently curled around her

wrist, effectively preventing her from using both arms to cover herself. 'In the flesh . . . sitting on your bed, waiting for me to put on a shirt and go have a beer with him.' His gaze suddenly dropped. Abbie yanked her arm free and returned it to guard-duty.

'Did you know your entire body is the colour of a beet?' he asked conversationally, which of course caused her blush to intensify.

'The water's hot. Will you please leave, so I can take my bath?' Mal ignored the request. A devilish, damnably sexy grin claimed his mouth as he leaned towards her. Abbie swallowed nervously. 'Now, Garrett . . .'

He brought his lips close to her ear to murmur, 'I'm glad you're not a bleached blonde.'

'How do you know——' she began, then broke off and closed her eyes in embarrassment. That was a mistake, because when his warm, firm lips settled on hers the sensation was all the more devastating.

The kiss was hard and passionate, but all too brief. Abbie opened her eyes in time to see him moving towards the door.

'I don't know how long this will take,' he said as he put it on. 'If I'm lucky, Tony will start talking after a few beers.'

'About the car, you mean?' Abbie asked.

He gave her an exasperated look. 'What else would I want him to talk about, for pity's sake?'

'Roxanne,' she suggested with a shrug.

He made a derisive sound in the back of his throat. 'Not likely. Besides, Tony couldn't tell me anything about Roxie Winston that I haven't already learned the hard way. If you still want that hot meal after you've had your bath, we'll be in the lounge.' He opened the door, then paused and looked back. 'I wasn't kidding before—you really could fall asleep in the tub. Don't stay in there too long, OK?'

Abbie smiled up at him. The pleasurable warmth that suffused her owed more to his concern than to the bath water. 'OK,' she said softly.

After he had gone she lay back and thought about what a complex, paradoxical, utterly fascinating man he was. Then she thought about the article she had made a firm commitment to write. By the time she climbed out of the tub and reached for a towel, she had decided on an entirely new angle for the piece. Roger probably wouldn't be thrilled—he was expecting an action-packed story about the race—but she thought she could work out a solution that would pacify him.

She pulled on jeans and a blouse, then collected her steno pad and quickly filled three pages with densely packed notes. She was still seated at the desk fifteen minutes later when a series of imperative knocks shattered her concentration. Abbie considered ignoring the summons, but then it occurred to her that Mal might have forgotten to take the room key with him when he left. Just in case, she closed the notebook and stuffed it back into her suitcase before going to open the door.

Roxanne Winston was the last person she had expected to find standing on the other side of it. Her initial surprise was quickly replaced by jealous suspicion.

'If you're looking for Mal, he isn't here,' she said coolly.

'I know,' Roxanne replied. 'I saw him leave with Tony. May I come in?'

Abbie was torn. Part of her—the cautious part—knew it was crazy to spend any more time in Roxanne's company than was absolutely necessary, especially looking as she did now—without make-up and wearing a simple shirt and jeans. But, as it often did, her curiosity overrode the instinctive urge for caution. Obviously Roxanne had come to see her. About what? That was the question of the hour. She stepped back and held the door open wide.

'By all means.'

Roxanne glided into the room and took time to make a leisurely inspection of its contents before turning to face her.

'I see you have two beds.'

Abbie forced her mouth to form a tight smile. 'It was the only room available when we checked in.' She casually took a seat on the bed closest to the door—the one with the noticeably rumpled spread—and felt a slash of malicious satisfaction when Roxanne's gaze travelled beyond her and her ice-blue eyes suddenly narrowed with displeasure. 'Won't you sit down?' Abbie murmured, indicating the desk chair.

Roxanne gave an impatient shake of her head. 'What I have to say won't take long. Mal's probably told you about us, about how I used him.'

'If you mean how you stole his design for the artificial heart and passed it off as your own,' Abbie said bluntly, 'yes, he told me.'

Roxanne neither denied the charge nor attempted to defend herself. 'It was a stupid move,' she said with surprising candour. 'If only I'd been patient a little longer, waited until he'd finished refining the design, he probably would have shared the credit with me. But I was young and ambitious, and frankly I just couldn't tolerate living in Hicksville any longer.' She laughed contemptuously. 'A big night out was dinner at Glady's Café followed by bingo at the church annexe.'

One slender manicured hand dismissed the town and its citizens with a single brusque gesture. 'But I'm sure you're familiar with what passes for a social life in rural Oklahoma. At any rate, the design for the heart was just a means to an end.'

'Your ticket to fame and fortune,' Abbie remarked.
Either her sarcasm went right by Roxanne, or she chose
to ignore it.

'Exactly. I told you I was ambitious. I still am.
Fortunately, I'm also extremely talented.'

'But not as talented as Mal,' Abbie murmured. 'If you
were, you wouldn't have had to steal his design to launch
your own career, and you wouldn't be using this race to
try to manipulate him into becoming your partner.'

Roxanne was clearly disconcerted by her perception.
For just an instant her sophisticated poise deserted her,
but then her gaze sharpened, became shrewdly assessing.
Abbie endured her scrutiny in anxious silence. It had
belatedly occurred to her that this was probably one of
those times when discretion would have been the better
part of something or other. With each second that passed
the probability that Roxanne would recognise her
increased.

'Well, well,' Roxanne finally drawled. 'Apparently
you're *not* just another dumb blonde.'

Abbie stifled her instinctive caustic response. While
telling the bitch off undoubtedly would have given her an
enormous amount of personal satisfaction, she couldn't
afford to indulge herself. Not yet; not until the race was
over.

'Why don't you say what you came to say, and then
leave?' she said with a bored indifference that was one
hundred per cent sham.

Roxanne stiffened slightly. 'All right. I intend to have
Mal back, and not just as a business partner.'

Abbie's lips quirked in a satiric smile. 'I think Mal
might have something to say about that. In case you
haven't noticed, you're not on the list of people he
admires most.'

Roxanne's dark head inclined slightly in

acknowledgement. 'Oh, I know he claims to despise me. He may even believe it. But no matter how he feels about me personally, Malachi Garrett's word is his bond. He's never welshed on a bet in his life and he won't welsh on this one. A week from now he'll be in New York, working side by side with me nine or ten hours a day, five, maybe six days a week. Even if you come with him, he'll spend more time with me than with you. I'll make sure he realises how much we have in common, how important the contacts I've made will be to his career. I'll be filled with remorse about the heartless way I used him three years ago and desperate to earn his forgiveness. Before the month is out he'll be back in my bed, and within three months we'll be married.'

Abbie could hardly believe the woman's conceit. Apparently it hadn't even occurred to her that Mal might be just a bit reluctant to succumb to her charms a second time.

'I hope for your sake that you haven't already mailed the wedding invitations,' she commented drily.

Roxanne's classically sculpted features tautened, her expression becoming overtly hostile. 'I'm warning you, Miss Kincaid, don't get in my way. I can be a real bitch when I'm crossed.'

'I know,' Abbie replied with a composure that severely taxed her self-control. 'Mal told me.' Deciding to end this confrontation before it turned into a hair-pulling contest, she gracefully rose to her feet. 'I think we've both made our positions clear. We could stand here and snipe at each other for the rest of the night, but it wouldn't accomplish anything. The bottom line is that you'll have to win the bet to get another shot at Mal. And frankly, Ms Winston, I don't think you have a chance in hell.'

She forced herself to walk calmly to the door. 'I'll have to ask you to leave now,' she said as she opened it. 'My lover is waiting for me to join him for a late supper.'

After Roxanne stalked out in a silent rage Abbie close
the door and leaned against it for a minute or so, waitin
for her own anger to subside. Then she put on her shoe
and headed for the lounge.

CHAPTER TWELVE

THE lounge was fairly crowded, but Abbie spotted him right away. He and Tony were sitting together at the bar, drinking beer straight from dark brown bottles. For some reason Mal glanced around just as she started toward him. A slow smile spread over his ruggedly handsome face and he swivelled his stool to face her. When Abbie reached him, he slid an arm around her waist and casually pulled her between his legs, then just as casually kissed her hello. Her total lack of response made him frown.

'Looks like the stag party's over,' Tony drawled from the next stool. 'Guess I'll call it a night.'

Abbie turned within the circle of Mal's arm. 'Please don't leave on my account. I won't be staying.'

He shook his head with a grin as he slid off the stool. 'Just teasin', Miss Abigail. I was leaving anyway—have to check in with the Dragon Lady. If I don't, she'll probably come looking for me.' He reached for her hand and shook it, his grip firm. 'Good luck, you two. See you at the Capitol.'

'He's a nice man,' Abbie observed as she watched Tony leave.

Mal turned her to face him. His hands rested lightly at her waist, but his thighs closed until they held her pelvis in a secure grip. 'I'm a nice man, too.'

'You have your moments,' she conceded with a noticeable lack of enthusiasm. 'How long have you and Tony known each other?'

'Practically all our lives. His dad owns the feed and grain store in town. We grew up together.' His hands shifted to her back and discovered the taut muscles there. He tried to pull her closer. Abbie stiffened in resistance. 'What's wrong?' he asked, frowning.

'Your friend the Dragon Lady just paid me a visit.'

Mal swore under his breath. Then he looked at her closely for the first time since she'd arrived, taking in the angry set of her jaw and the stormy green of her irises.

'Let's move to a table,' he said, clasping her hand as he vacated the bar stool. 'We'll order that hot meal I owe you, but first I suspect you could use a drink.'

When they were both seated at a small corner table and a waitress had taken their order, he scooted his chair next to hers so that he could drape his arm over her shoulders.

'Do you have to sit so close?' Abbie complained.'

'Yes,' he said firmly. 'It's obvious that Roxie put a bee in your bonnet about something, and now you're using whatever she said as an excuse to give me the cold shoulder. But if you think I'll let you freeze me out, Abigail Prudence Kincaid, you can think again. We both know I can melt that iceberg you're hiding behind.' His voice suddenly deepened. His fingers toyed with her earlobe. 'Want me to prove it?'

Fortunately the waitress chose that moment to return with their drink order—a Tom Collins and another bottle of beer. Abbie snatched at the tall, frosty glass as if she'd just spent a month in the desert.

Mal let her take a couple of long sips, then removed the drink from her hand and set it back on the table. 'Take it easy,' he drawled. 'Let's get some food in your stomach before you finish that off. I want you thawed, not pickled.'

'What makes you think I give a damn what you want?'

she replied crossly.

He leaned closer, his breath a soft caress against her cheek. 'Because you want the same two things,' he said in a husky murmur. 'To beat Roxanne and for us to make love, not necessarily in that order. Tell me I'm wrong.'

Abbie wished she could. She turned her head to give him a resentful look. His warm, intimate gaze was waiting to capture and hold hers. Her heart knocked against her ribs. Breathing suddenly required a conscious effort. 'You're not wrong,' she heard herself murmur.

Desire flared in Mal's eyes. He leaned closer still, his fingers slipping into her hair as he started to tilt her head back. Abbie's lips parted in anticipation. But then he suddenly seemed to remember where they were. His hand dropped back to her shoulder and he inhaled a deep, ragged breath as he retreated several inches.

'What were we talking about?' he asked roughly.

The angry tension that had gripped Abbie since she left their room suddenly melted away. 'Roxanne,' she said with a tiny smile.

Mal grimaced and reached for his beer. 'Right. Roxanne. So, what did she say that put you in such a rotten mood?'

'Where to begin?' she said drily. 'For one thing, she informed me that she intends to be Mrs Malachi Garrett within three months.'

Mal's bottle slammed down on the table so hard that beer spurted out the top. 'The hell she does!'

'She also warned me not to get in her way. She said she can be a real bitch when she's crossed.'

His mouth twisted in derision. 'That may be the only honest claim she's made in years. Damn the woman! I'm sorry, Abigail. If I hadn't come out with Tony, she wouldn't have had a chance to corner you.'

'It wasn't your fault,' Abbie told him. The waitress

arrived with her steak dinner. She waited until the woman had returned to her station, then added, 'Anyway, our little skirmish wasn't entirely one-sided. I managed to get in a couple of shots.'

'I'll bet you did,' Mal said with a grin. 'Since I didn't have a ringside seat, why don't you give me a blow-by-blow account.'

'Forget it,' she said emphatically as she removed his arm from her shoulders. 'It's your turn to talk. You can tell me what you found out from Tony while I devour this steak.'

What he'd found out from Tony was encouraging. Roxanne's engine wasn't performing as well as she'd expected. So far they had made three stops for minor adjustments. Each adjustment had improved the engine's fuel-efficiency, but Roxanne still wasn't satisfied.

'Did he say what kind of mileage they're getting?' Abbie asked between bites.

'He claimed they're averaging fifty-six miles per gallon, but I suspect he was fudging a little. The actual figure is probably closer to sixty-six.'

'Even if you're right, we're still using less than they are,' she pointed out. 'Assuming we don't have any problems between here and Washington, you would win the bet.'

'Right,' Mal said, but he didn't sound as convinced as Abbie would have liked. She finished the last of her baked potato and sat back to study him. The creases between his eyebrows had reappeared, a sure sign that something was troubling him.

'What's wrong?' she asked in concern.

'I wish I knew,' he said irritably. 'The engine's performing even better than I expected. Our mileage figures are terrific and we're ahead of schedule, time-wise.'

'But?' Abbie prompted.

His shoulders moved in a restless shrug. 'Maybe I'm just being neurotic, but I can't shake the feeling that we're due for some bad luck. Things have been going too well.'

Abbie impulsively reached for his hand. 'If it would make you feel better, I could slip out while you're asleep tonight and sabotage the car,' she teased. 'Unfortunately I wouldn't have any idea what wires to pull loose or anything technical like that, but I could turn on the headlights so the battery would be dead in the morning.'

Mal couldn't quite suppress a smile. 'You'd really do that for me? I'm touched.'

'It wouldn't be any trouble,' she assured him.

His smile spread to his eyes and he curled his fingers around hers, imprisoning her hand in a warm, possessive grip. 'Do you want dessert?'

His voice was suddenly deeper, rougher. As Abbie watched, mesmerised, the warm glow in his eyes became a flickering golden flame.

'No,' she said in a breathless whisper.

He lifted her hand to his mouth and gently bit the heel of her thumb. 'What do you want?'

For a moment Abbie forgot how to breathe. She closed her eyes, hoping that if she didn't look at him she would be able to resist temptation. Then his tongue stabbed at the centre of her palm. She gasped in reaction.

'Tell me,' he murmured insistently. 'Open your eyes and look at me, and tell me what you want.'

Her lashes fluttered against her cheeks as she made a last-ditch effort to resist the inevitable. When she reluctantly opened her eyes, the heat and hunger she saw in his destroyed the last remaining trace of her will-power.

'You.'

Apparently it was the answer Mal had been after. He

shot out of his chair, pulling her up with him, jarring the table in his haste, then paused a moment to dig into his pocket for a couple of bills, which he tossed down without bothering to check the denominations. He only stopped long enough to pay the cashier. As soon as they were outside, he scooped Abbie up in his arms.

'Mal?' she said breathlessly, hastily hooking an arm around his neck.

'What?' They rounded the corner at the rear of the building. He stepped over a small hedge without breaking stride.

'Do you realise that you left the waitress a forty-dollar tip?'

He didn't respond, walking right through the middle of a bed of geraniums, evidently determined to take the shortest possible route to their room even if it meant demolishing a few flower-beds along the way.

'You said we wouldn't make love tonight,' Abbie reminded him.

'I changed my mind.'

'Oh. Well, being carried off into the night like this is very romantic and all, but I'd appreciate a few kisses, at least, before we fall into bed.'

He glanced down at her, his expression grim. 'If I kiss you know, we'll never make it to the room.'

Abbie tried to swallow, but her mouth was too dry. 'In that case, I guess I can wait,' she said in a voice she scarcely recognised as her own.

When they reached the door he set her firmly down to fish in his pocket for the room key, swearing softly but savagely when he couldn't immediately locate it, then seized her wrist and hauled her inside. Abbie almost tripped over the threshold. The door slammed shut. She stood in the darkness beside it for all of two seconds before his hands found her and dragged her against him.

The instant before his mouth would have crashed down on hers, she turned her head, pressing her cheek to his shoulder.

'Please . . . you're scaring me.'

The timid admission slipped out of her all on its own. Abbie thought it couldn't possibly have surprised Mal any more than it had surprised her. She held her breath while she waited for his reaction.

One of his hands lifted to her head, his touch suddenly gentle. 'Am I?' he murmured hoarsely.

She nodded. 'A little.'

His chest expanded as he drew a deep, uneven breath. 'Were you telling the truth when you said you were twenty-three before you made love for the first time?'

Abbie grimaced. 'If I'd wanted to lie, I'd have said I was eighteen or nineteen,' she told him drily.

Mal's fingers slipped into her hair and began to rake through it lightly, almost absently. 'How old are you now?'

'Twenty-five,' she murmured with a frown. 'What's that got to do with anything?'

He ignored the question. 'And how many men have there been since that first time?'

'Are you writing a book?'

She said it exactly the same way he had, when she'd questioned him about Roxanne. Mal also repeated her response, but with a thread of lazy amusement running through his deep voice.

'No, just curious. Are you going to answer the question?'

'One,' Abbie muttered reluctantly.

'And I'd be willing to bet they were both perfect gentlemen,' he drawled. 'Polite, well-mannered——'

'Considerate,' she put in with a smile.

'Dull.'

'Gallant.'

'Predictable, boring three-piece suits. Well, I'm none of those things, Abigail. I can be as considerate as the next man, but I'm seldom predictable and I almost never bother to be polite. And as for gallant . . . hell, I'm not even sure what it means, but if somebody accused me of being gallant when I had a few beers under my belt, I'd probably punch him in the mouth.'

Abbie closed her eyes and slipped her arms around his waist. 'What are you trying to tell me, Garrett—that you're not a gentleman?'

'Not on my best day,' he muttered. 'You said that when you see something you want, you go after it. So do I, and what I want right now, more than anything, is to make love to you. A gentleman might have taken you for a stroll in the moonlight, maybe stolen a few kisses before he tried to manipulate you into bed. Sorry, darlin', but that's not my style.' He paused a moment, then murmured huskily, 'Now the question is, would you rather go to bed with a nice, polite three-piece suit, or with a rude, crude male chauvinist pig who promises to love you like you've never been loved before?'

Abbie answered by stretching up to kiss him. She was boldly aggressive, communicating her preference in a language far more eloquent than words would have been. Mal returned the kiss, but that was all. She could feel the control he was exerting in every rigidly tense line of his body. The laboured rhythm of his heart against her breasts and the occasional shudder that rippled through him told her how much that control was costing him. She pulled back enough to whisper, 'In case there's any doubt left in your mind, I want you, Malachi Garrett, not some boring old three-piece suit.'

'Are you still afraid?' he asked hoarsely against her lips. She shook her head. 'I know you wouldn't do anything

America's Favorite Author

Janet
DAILEY

SWEET
PROMISE

One kiss—a sweet promise
of a hunger long denied

SWEET PROMISE

*E*rica was starved for love. Daughter of a Texas
millionaire who had time only for business, she'd
thought up a desperate scheme to get her father's
attention.

Unfortunately her plan backfired and she found herself
seriously involved with Rafael de la Torres, a man she
believed to be a worthless fortune hunter.

That had been a year ago; the affair had almost ruined
her life. Now she was in love with a wonderful man.
But she wasn't free to marry him. First of all she must
find Rafael . . .!

Janet
DAILEY

to hurt me. It was just that you . . . took me by surprise.'

His ragged sigh seemed to drain the tension from his body. His hands shifted, gathering her closer so that the hard evidence of his arousal pressed into her stomach.

'Well, darlin', just so I don't give you any more nasty surprises——' he bent his head to murmur in her ear —this is what's going to happen next . . .'

Some of the things he whispered should have made Abbie blush from head to toe. She did in fact quickly become flushed with heat, but she didn't delude herself that the sudden dilation of every capillary in her body had anything to do with embarrassment. He roused wants and needs she hadn't been aware she possessed, calling forth a primitive, sensual part of her that had, until now, lain dormant.

By the time they had finished undressing each other and moved on to the bed, not a single inhibition or reservation remained. Her inquisitive hands and mouth stroked, rubbed, tasted and explored with eager abandon, until a tortured groan erupted from Mal's chest and he reached out to stop her.

'No more,' he said in a thick voice totally unlike his normal lazy drawl. 'Dear God, Abbie, how much do you think one man can take?'

She ducked her head and bit his shoulder, then loitered to run the top of her tongue along the tiny indentations her teeth had made. 'That's the first time you've called me Abbie.'

'If you don't stop teasing me, it may be the last time I call you anything,' he gasped. 'Because I'll be either unconscious or dead.'

Abbie lifted her head, finding his mouth by instinct in the dark. 'I'm not teasing,' she whispered as her hands glided down his body.'

A sound that was part moan, part growl and all male

rumbled up from his chest and into her mouth as hi
arms locked around her and he rolled, pinning he
beneath him. Abbie clasped him to her with a
eagerness that made his head spin, welcoming hi
strong, gliding thrust with a tiny cry of joy, calling hi
name between gasps and whimpers and soft moans o
ecstasy.

Their loving was fierce and frantic and utterl
satisfying. As soon as Mal was able to move he eased on
to his back, taking Abbie with him. Her head settled on
his shoulder, one slender hand coming to rest over hi
heart. He stroked her hair and she felt him place a kis
on the top of her head.

'Are you all right?' he asked. The slight catch in hi
voice told her that the ferocity of their passion had
shaken him as much as it had her.

'I think so,' she murmured. Her own voice was fa
from steady. 'Ask me again in a week. It'll take me a
least that long to recuperate.'

A husky chuckle accompanied Mal's one-armed hug
'I hate to burst your balloon, darlin', but I suspect that
week from now we'll both be in cardiac intensive care.

Abbie fell asleep before she could think of a suitabl
reply.

He woke her just before dawn, his hands and mout
coaxing her out of a deep, dreamless sleep. Thei
lovemaking was slow, achingly tender and piercingl
sweet, and as completely satisfying as it had been th
first time. They fell asleep in a tangle of limbs an
bedclothes, and didn't wake again until almost ten. Ma
jumped out of bed and started gathering the clothe
they'd discarded in such haste the night before, cursin
himself for not remembering to order a wake-up call an
muttering dire predictions that Roxanne and Tony wer
probably half-way to Washington by now. When Abbi

informed him that she wasn't going anywhere until she'd had a shower, he grumbled and complained, cursed some more, and then—when she climbed out from beneath the sheet and stretched luxuriously—did an abrupt about-face and decided to join her. When they emerged from the bathroom they were still running late, but he was in a much better mood.

While Abbie checked to make sure they hadn't forgotten anything, Mal collected their luggage and carried it out to the car. His enraged bellow brought her running to the door. She saw the reason for his fury at once.

Both tyres on the driver's side of the Shelby were as flat as pancakes.

CHAPTER THIRTEEN

'The bitch!'

In the first minute or so after he discovered the flats, those were the only words Mal uttered that didn't turn the air blue. Abbie hurried around the car to check the other two tyres.

'The ones on this side are OK,' she reported.

'Of course,' he said flatly. 'The Sable was parked on that side. She wouldn't have wanted Tony to know about her dirty little trick.'

He lifted the hood to check for additional signs of sabotage and said a word that made Abbie wince.

'What else?' she asked anxiously.

He held up a long strip of rubber. 'Fan belt.'

'Broken?'

'Cut,' Mal said tersely. He stuck his head back under the hood and announced that two fuses were also missing. 'She wasn't taking any chances,' he muttered as he removed his cap to rake a hand through his hair.;

'How bad is it?' Abbie asked. 'I mean, how long will it take to pump up the tyres and replace the belt and the fuses?'

He leaned against the Shelby's fender and considered the problem. 'I brought a few spare fuses, just in case one blew, and there's probably a service station nearby that has a portable compressed air tank. If it was a weekday, could make one phone call and have the fan belt delivered in a matter of minutes. But this is Sunday. God knows how long it'll take to find an auto parts store

164

that's open.'

'Then we'd better start making calls,' Abbie suggested.

Mal straightened and closed the hood. 'First let's check with the manager. If he lives around here, he can probably narrow down the list of places we should try and hopefully save us some time.'

The day manager turned out to be a young woman, and it just so happened that her cousin's husband's brother was the parts manager for a local Ford dealership. She called him at home, briefly explained the situation and then handed the phone to Mal. When he hung up, the man had agreed to deliver a new fan belt within the hour.

'He's bringing a portable air tank, too,' he told Abbie as they walked away from the desk.

She went into the restaurant just off the lobby and ordered two sausage and pancake breakfasts to take away while Mal went to replace the missing fuses. When she returned to the car he was sitting inside it, the calculator balanced on one knee and a spiral notebook on the other. The door to their room was still standing open. Abbie carried the bag containing their breakfasts inside and unpacked two coffees, two orange juices, two styrofoam food containers and two sets of plastic utensils. Mal appeared in the doorway just as she finished setting everything out on the desk.

'I wondered where you'd disappeared to,' he said. 'What's that?'

'Breakfast. Come and eat before it gets cold.'

He inspected his hands and decided he'd better wash them first. On the way to the bathroom he paused to give her a lingering kiss. 'You're gonna make some man a dandy little wife, Abigail Prudence,' he said in an exaggerated drawl.

'Not likely,' she muttered.

Mal had already entered the bathroom and turned on the water, so Abbie didn't think he'd heard. Just as well, she thought dismally. She would prefer not to be called upon to explain the remark. After last night, it was impossible to convince herself that she wasn't head over heels in love with him. It was equally impossible to sell herself on the idea that he might eventually forgive her for the way she'd deceived and used him. And, since very few men married women they despised, it didn't seem likely that there were any orange blossoms or wedding bells looming on her horizon.

Telling herself that there was no point in dwelling on such negative thoughts, she started wrestling an armchair across the floor to the desk. She'd managed to drag it about three feet when Mal's hand suddenly grasped her upper arms and he gently moved her aside.

'What do you have against marriage?' he asked, hefting the chair as if it were a box of Kleenex.

Abbie tried to exude sophisticated nonchalance. 'Nothing. I just don't want to be a wife.'

Mal waited until she was comfortably situated in the armchair before he sat down beside her. She couldn't help thinking that he displayed very nice manners for a man who rarely bothered to be polite.

'Heaven knows, I'm no expert,' he drawled, 'but I've always thought that when two people got married, one became a husband and the other became a wife.'

'Which is exactly why so many marriages end in divorce,' she said as she opened the plastic container of maple syrup and dumped it on her pancakes. 'If I ever do get married, I'll hire somebody to be the wife.'

Mal cocked his head, his expression quizzical. 'Are you saying you'd pay another woman to sleep with your husband?'

'Of course not! I'm talking about hiring somebody to do all the dreary, thankless chores that wives get stuck with—washing, ironing, scrubbing pots and pans, cleaning the house moss out from under the beds and the cobwebs off the ceilings . . . that kind of thing.'

'Thank heavens,' he muttered. 'I thought this was some goofy new feminist craze—surrogate wives, or something like that.'

Abbie gave him a speaking look, but she refused to be drawn into an argument about feminism. 'You know what I mean,' she said after a moment. 'Nine times out of ten the woman gets saddled with all the stuff that's jsut plain drudgery, while hubby goes off to play golf or tennis or whatever.'

'You're right,' he said, surprising her. 'But I don't think hiring a "wife" is the answer. Has it occurred to you that if you married a man who was already accustomed to keeping house for himself, the problem probably wouldn't arise in the first place? You could divide the housework and then *both* go off to play golf or tennis or whatever.'

'Great idea,' she said drily. 'Unfortunately, men like that are as scarce as hen's teeth. At least, heterosexual men under the age of fifty. If you know one, point me to him.'

Mal wiped his mouth with a paper napkin, then sat back and tapped his chest. 'You're looking at one,' he said with a lop-sided grin.

Abbie choked on a sip of orange juice.

He jumped up and quickly moved behind her chair. 'That's not a very flattering reaction,' he drawled as he whacked her between the shoulder-blades.

She struggled to clear her windpipe and think of something to say, in that order. The former was accomplished fairly easily. The latter proved to be much

more difficult. She coughed a few more times to give
herself another couple of seconds.

There was a tentative knock at the door, which Mal
had left open, followed by a man's voice asking, "Scuse
me, but do y'all belong to the black Cobra with the
busted fan belt?'

'That's us,' Mal answered. 'I'll be with you in a
minute.' He bent over and stared into Abbie's tear-
drenched eyes. 'You going to be OK?'

She nodded vigorously and waved him away. When
he'd followed the man outside she wilted with relief,
grateful that she had a minute or two of privacy in which
to recover from the shock he'd given her.

'You're looking at one.' What on earth had he meant
by that? Surely he hadn't been presenting himself for
consideration. Had he? The thought alone was enough
to make her heart palpitate.

'Get serious, Abigail,' she muttered as she started
clearing away the remains of their late breakfast. He had
been teasing her again, that was all—joking, kidding
around. It would be absurd to imagine anything else.

They made one short stop to fill the tank and were back
on the interstate a few minutes past noon. Abbie didn't
bother to consult Mal about their speed. Conscious of
how much time they'd already lost, she accelerated
steadily until the speedometer registered ninety miles
per hour, then maintained that speed all the way to
Charleston, West Virginia. Fortunately the radar
detector remained silent for the entire two hundred and
fifty-nine miles.

They had left behind the relatively flat terrain of the
Midwestern plains. As they travelled eastwards the land
rose in a series of progressively steeper hills, with lush
green valleys nestled between their slopes. It was a

particularly beautiful part of the country, and Abbie regretted the fact that they couldn't spare the time to stop occasionally and spend a few minutes just admiring the scenery.

The sky over Louisville had been sprinkled with high, fluffy white clouds. By the time they reached Charleston the clouds had formed a dense, low-hanging mass, its dirty grey belly ominously close and heavy-looking. Every few minutes thunder rumbled overhead.

'Looks like we're in for a gully-washer,' Mall remarked.

Abbie glanced at him in concern. 'Should we stop, or keep going and hope we can outrun it?'

'I'd rather keep going, unless you need a break. How are you holding up?'

'Fine,' she said truthfully. 'I should be OK for another hour or two. We'll be coming to the interchange for I79 before long. Maybe we'll leave this stuff behind once we head north.'

Unfortunately, such was not the case. Five minutes later it was raining so hard that Abbie turned on the headlights and reduced their speed to sixty, and then fifty. While she concentrated on keeping the car between the barely visible white lines, Mal kept his eyes peeled for stalled or slow-moving vehicles ahead.

For the next hundred and twenty miles they averaged between thirty and forty miles per hour. Wind-whipped sheets of rain blasted the Shelby from every direction, and in places the road was covered by almost a foot of water. The windows quickly fogged up, which meant the defroster had to be run continuously. Even with the fan on high, Mal had to clear the windscreen with a tissue or a paper napkin every two or three minutes. Before long the interior of the car began to feel like a sauna.

'I'm beginning to think we should have stopped at that

last rest area,' Abbie said as an especially strong gust of wind nudged them on to the shoulder of the road. She steered to the left to compensate, barely managing to keep the tyres on the road.

They had passed two rest areas, the last one about forty miles back. The parking areas of both had been crowded with cars, trucks and vans.

Mal nodded as he leaned over to wipe away the condensation on her side of the windshield. 'Apparently everybody but us had sense enough to pull over and wait this thing out. How are you doing?'

'Don't ask,' she said with a grimace. 'I've discovered that at any speed below fifty your wonder-car handles like a log wagon.'

He reached out to gently tuck a lock of hair behind her ear. 'Next time we make a trip like this, I'll be sure to provide you with power steering.'

The promise was made casually, and yet he sounded completely serious, as if he took it for granted that they would be making more trips together. Abbie felt like crying. She smiled wanly, not trusting her voice.

A few miles later they came to another rest area. This one was deserted. Evidently no one else had been brave enough or foolhardy enough to press on this far. Abbie parked as close to the shelterhouse as possible. Mal rolled up the atlas and shoved it into her shoulder-bag, then they made a mad dash across the small lake that had formed in front of the building. They were both soaked to the skin by the time they ducked under the roof.

Abbie pushed her dripping hair back from her face, then took a look around. There were vending machines for soft drinks and snack foods, public restrooms, a couple of drinking fountains and that was it.

'Not exactly the Ritz, but at leat the roof doesn't leak,' Mal commented as he wandered over to a huge map of the state hanging on one wall. 'According to this, we only have about twenty miles to go before we hit highway forty-eight. From there it's just a hop, skip and a jump to I70.'

Abbie removed the road atlas from her shoulder-bag and opened it to the page for West Virginia. 'Your hop, skip and a jump looks more like a hundred and ten or twenty miles to me,' she said drily. 'And a fairly long stretch of it's only two-lane.'

She continued to study the atlas while Mal went to examine the vending machines. He returned a minute later with two cans of root beer and two bags of pretzels. Abbie rerolled the atlas and stuck it back in her bag to take one of each.

'Join me for lunch?' he invited, dropping down to sit on the floor, his back against the wall.

Her knee joints protested as she eased down beside him. 'In case you hadn't noticed, it's almost six-thirty.'

'OK, we'll call it an early supper.'

Abbie hadn't realised how hungry she was until she bit off half of the first pretzel. She made herself eat slowly, though. There was no telling how long it would be before they found an honest-to-goodness restaurant that served real food. By the time she'd finished the last salty crumb, the storm seemed to have diminished to a common, ordinary downpour.

When she returned from a trip to the ladies' room, Mal was feeding change into the soft drink machine. There were several bags of pretzels and corn chips and half a dozen chocolate bars piled on top of it.

'You must have been even hungrier than I was,' she said in amusement.

He glanced around and grinned at her. 'I decided we might as well stock up while we've got the chance. Do you have any quarters?'

She found room in her bag for four canned drinks and the chocolate bars. Mal stuffed the cellophane bags inside his shirt. When they were ready to dash back to the car, he requested the keys.

'Do you need to get something out of the back?' Abbie asked as she dug in the crowded shoulder-bag for the key-ring.

'No,' he replied. 'I'm going to drive for a while.'

At first she thought he was kidding. By the time she realised he wasn't, her hand was extended towards him, the key ring lying in the middle of her palm. She quickly closed her fingers around it.

'You? Drive?' She made each word a separate question, as if they had no business being part of the same sentence.

Mal looked slightly affronted. 'It is my car,' he reminded her.

'I know it's your car, but you admitted back at the farm that you're the worst driver west of the Mississippi.'

'Those were Deke's words,' he said impatiently. 'I only admitted to being a lousy driver. The keys, Abigail.'

Abbie hesitated a moment, but the determined glint in his eyes suggested that if she didn't give them to him he would take them. She handed them over reluctantly. 'I hope you know what you're doing,' she muttered. 'I'm warning you, Garrett—if you drive us off the side of a mountain, I'll never speak to you again.'

His blinding smile was an unexpected as the light kiss he dropped on the end of her nose. 'Don't be such a worrywart, darlin'. I haven't driven off a mountain in ages.'

When they climbed back into the car, the windows were shrouded in a mist of condensation. Abbie unpacked the soft drinks and chocolate bars from her shoulder-bag, dumping everything on the floor behind her seat, and fished out an enormous wad of paper towels. Mal tossed the bags of pretzels and corn chips on top of the pile she'd made, then rebuttoned his shirt and adjusted the driver's seat to accommodate his longer legs.

'Where'd you get the towels?' he asked in surprise.

'From the ladies' room.'

He shook his head, an affectionate smile tugged at the corners of his sensual mouth. 'Beautiful, smart *and* practical. That settles it, Abigail. I'm going to have to keep you.'

Abbie felt as if a giant fist had her heart in a stranglehold. She blindly thrust a handful of towels at him as she turned away. 'Here,' she muttered. 'You clear your side and I'll clear mine.'

Mal took the towels without speaking. In fact, neither of them said anything for quite some time. Abbie was so miserable that she could summon neither the desire nor the energy to make idle conversation. The article she'd promised Roger was a burden she'd have given anything to be rid of. Her mood and the weather were in perfect harmony—gloomy and grey, with not a ray of sunshine in sight.'

She was so absorbed in her own unhappiness that she forgot to worry about Mal's driving until they passed a sign alerting motorists that the junction for highway forty-eight was one mile ahead. At the same time, she noticed that the downpour had decreased to a drizzle.

'The turn-off for forty-eight is coming up,' she mentioned casually, trying to be tactful, not wanting to come right out and tell him that she would feel a lot more comfortable if he turned control of the car back over to her.

'Mm-hmm,' he murmured. 'How about opening a can of root beer for me?'

Abbie twisted around to locate and retrieve one of the cans. 'You know, you really shouldn't drink it while you're driving. Why don't you pull over and we'll trade places for a while?'

He slanted her a drily amused look. 'Stop worrying, Abigail. I haven't driven us off the side of a mountain yet, have I?'

Abbie pulled the ring tab on the can and passed it to him along with a perturbed look. For the next hour she paid close attention to his driving. She didn't observe anything to find fault with. In fact he seemed to be a very skilled, conscientious driver, always alert to conditions around him, yet completely relaxed. She fetched a can of lemonade for herself and sipped at it with a puzzled frown.

'Why did you tell me you're a lousy driver?' Her tone made it as much an accusation as a question.

Mal shrugged. 'Maybe lousy was the wrong word to use.'

'Then what would be the right word?'

He thought a moment, his lips pursed. 'Reckless, I suppose.'

Abbie's gaze darted to the guard rail at the edge of the highway and the steep drop-off beyond it. 'Reckless?' she repeated, trying not to sound alarmed. 'How do you mean?'

'I tend to take too many unnecessary chances.' His tone was so matter-of-fact that she glanced at him sharply, wondering if he was putting her on, trying to scare her just for the hell of it.

'I guess it's a holdover from my racing days,' he added in the same offhand tone.

Abbie blinked in surprise. 'You used to race cars?' He was putting her on. He must be. Yet, now that she thought of it, he did have those helmets on a shelf in the garage . . .

'In my wild, misspent youth,' he confirmed. 'Tony, Dave Southfield and I used to compete on the dirt-track circuit. They were both better drivers, so I compensated by being more aggressive, taking more risks.'

Abbie stole another glance out the window. Her mouth went dry. There were clouds *below* them. 'You're telling me this *now*, when you're driving along an unfamiliar two-lane highway, in the rain, on top of a mountain, at——' She leaned over to look at the speedometer and gave a horrified gasp. 'We're doing almost sixty-five!'

Mal laughed softly. 'Calm down. The rain's almost stopped and there's no traffic to speak of. Besides, I didn't complain when you were whizzing along at ninety, did I?'

'We were on a four-lane interstate highway then,' she retorted. 'And *I* have never been accused of being a reckless driver. Never!'

'Believe me, darlin', I have no intention of endangering either of us,' Mal assured her. 'I've considered the weather and the condition of the road surface and I know how this car responds. Our speed is well below the maximum safe limit.' He gave her a reassuring smile. 'I'm carrying a very special passenger, whose health and safety I'm not about to risk just to win a stupid race.'

The warm sincerity in both his voice and his gaze soothed Abbie's anxiety and at the same time made her want to crawl under her seat and curl up in shame. He thought she was 'special'. What a laugh. She couldn't bear to think about what his opinion of her would be when he learned the truth.

They reached I70 without having glimpsed a single white Sable all day. Mal had Abbie take a flashlight out of the glove compartment and consult the atlas to find out how far they were from the interchange for I270, which led directly to Washington.

'It's another fifty-two miles,' she said as she bent over the map. 'And from there about thirty more to the beltway around the city.'

'There should be at least one motel close to the interchange,' Mal said. 'We can stop there for the night and zip on down to DC early tomorrow morning.'

As it happened, there were several motels near the interchange. Mal chose another Holiday Inn, for sentimental reasons, he said. This time he requested a double room. Abbie couldn't summon the strengtrh to deny herself one more night in his arms, even though she knew it would make his inevitable rejection even more painful. She would store up as many memories as she could tonight, and try very hard not to think about what tomorrow would bring.

'Do you like pizza?' Mal asked as he carried in their luggage.

She stopped in the middle of a joint-popping stretch to look at him in surprise. 'Sure. Doesn't everybody?'

He put the bags in the wardrobe as he had the night before. 'I saw a Noble Roman's down the road. How 'bout if I go pick up a pizza and we eat it here?'

'Fine,' Abbie murmured as she stifled a yawn.

'Are you sure? Because if you were looking forward to a sit-down meal in a nice restaurant, we can do that.'

She shook her head. 'No, I'm too bushed to go out. Pizza sounds great, really. A *large* pizza—Italian sausage and mushrooms, with extra peppers.'

'You got it.' He flashed a dazzling smile and started for the door, then suddenly stopped and turned back. His smile was no longer in evidence. 'There's something I want you to think about while I'm gone,' he said quietly. 'I've dropped some pretty broad hints today, most of which you've done a jim-dandy job of ignoring.'

He didn't have to be more specific. Abbie knew exactly

what 'hints' he referred to. His words whispered through her mind as she maintained a precarious balance between hope and dread.

You're gonna make some man a dandy little wife . . . You're looking at one . . . Next time we make a trip like this . . . I'm going to have to keep you . . .

She stared at him helplessly, not knowing how to respond.

'It finally dawned on me that maybe I wasn't getting the reaction I wanted because I was using the wrong approach,' he went on with a wry smile. 'You're a lady who says what's on her mind. No doubt you expect the same kind of honesty from a man. OK, no more beating around the bush.'

He paused, gazing at her with solemn intensity. 'I've fallen in love with you, Abigail Prudence Kincaid, and I think—I *hope*—you feel the same way about me.'

Abbie made an involuntary sound that was part joy and part despair.

'No, don't say anything!' Mal ordered. 'Just hear me out. When I go back to Oklahoma, I want you to come with me. I know you're a liberated, independent woman and I realise we'll both have to do some compromising, but I think we can make it work. I'm not asking for a long-term commitment. Not yet, anyway. You're not ready for that, and God knows I don't want to scare you off. Just think about it, that's all I ask. I don't want your answer until after this business with Roxie is finished. That gives you till noon tomorrow to decide.'

He turned and walked out without another word, leaving a pale and shaken Abbie standing in the middle of the room, staring dazedly at the door he'd closed behind him.

CHAPTER FOURTEEN

THE next half-hour was the longest of Abbie's life. It had taken her less than a minute to realise that she had to come clean and tell Mal everything. That had been the easy part. It was the waiting for him to return so she could get it over with, and the fearful anticipation of his reaction, that made the remaining twenty-nine minutes seem like twenty-nine hours. By the time she heard the distinctive growl of the Shelby's engine she had chewed her fingernails to the quick and eaten six antacid tablets.

Expecting him to use the room key, she was surprised when he knocked instead. She hurred to open the door and immediately saw why he hadn't let himself in. In addition to a large cardboard pizza box, he was holding a two-litre bottle of Coke and the oversized Sunday edition of a newspaper. He dropped a kiss on the end of her nose and then carried everything to the desk, glancing at her nails in surprise as she inspected the pizza inside the carton.

'I didn't know you bit your nails?'

'There's a lot about me you don't know,' she muttered as she closed the door.

Mal pulled a bunch of paper napkins out of his hip pocket and laid them next to the pizza box. 'No doubt,' he said mildly. 'Just as there are things about me that you don't know. Darn, I forgot to ask for cups. Would you get a couple of those plastic glasses from the bathroom?'

'Sure,' Abbie murmured. When she got into the

178

bathroom, she faced her own reflection in the mirror. Her shoulders drooped. She looked like something the cat had dragged in, her hair a matted snarl of curls framing a wan, drawn face in which the only feature with any life was a pair of apprehensive blue-green eyes.

She looked awful. The only time she'd ever looked worse was the winter she'd been flat on her back with the 'flu for two weeks. The prospect of spending the night with her should have sent any sane man running for the hills. And yet thirty minutes ago Mal had looked her square in the eyes and told her he'd fallen in love with her and wanted her to come back to Oklahoma with him. Malachi Garrett, the same man who had admitted that he distrusted all women—and for good reason—had actually said those things to her.

For the first time since he walked out the door, she let herself hope that he just might love her enough to forgive her deceit. Perhaps not right away, but in time. And she could wait, for however long it took. He was a man worth waiting for.

She squared her shoulders, picked up two of the small plastic glasses and went to make her confession. Mal was sitting on the bed, a section of the newspaper lying across his lap. He looked up, straight into her eyes, his expression solemn.

'There's a story on the front page that caught my eye while I was waiting for the pizza. I think you should read it.'

He spoke softly, his voice curiously devoid of emotion. Abbie's heart seemed to skip a beat, then started thudding heavily. She set the glasses on the desk and took the newspaper from his outstretched hand.

She found the story he meant right away. The headline read 'Experimental Engine Test Fails'; the dateline was Morgantown, West Virginia. As she scanned the sort, two-column story a weight seemed to lift from her shoulders. She sank down beside Mal, scarcely daring to believe what she was reading. When she reached the end of the second column, she turned to face him.

His intent, slightly sombre gaze remained focused on her as he sat stiffly upright on the edge of the mattress. The twin creases between his eyebrows had reappeared and there was a film of perspiration on his upper lip. Abbie knew that if she touched him his muscles would be bunched with tension. He seemed . . . *nervous* was the first word that came to mind. The idea was so ludicrous that she dismissed it at once.

'I'm sorry,' he said unexpectedly.

Abbie shook her head in confusion. 'Why should you be sorry? According to this, Roxanne's engine gave up the ghost somewhere in the mountains of West Virginia. You've *won*, Garrett! You should be thrilled.'

Mal nodded once, brusquely. 'Of course I'm pleased.'

'You don't look like it,' Abbie said bluntly. 'You look like you just got a notice that your tax return is being audited. What is it? Did I miss something?' She bent over the paper again and began to reread the story.

'Aren't you upset?' Mal demanded. He sounded as if he thought she should be. '*I'm* sure as hell upset.'

She lifted her head to give him a baffled frown. 'Upset about what?'

'That newspaper story, of course,' he said impatiently. 'By now all the media have probably picked it up. Chances are that every reporter in Washington will be waiting for us in front of the Capitol Building tomorrow morning.'

Abbie felt as if someone had whacked her in the centre of the chest with a sledge-hammer. Of course. How could she have forgotten his antagonism towards the Press

e was angry because somehow the story had been
aked, probably by Roxanne. By tomorrow evening his
me and face would be on the front page of every major
stern newspaper. Including the *Post*.

The hope she had allowed to blossom just minutes
fore withered and died, to be replaced by a cold, hard
ot of dread. 'There's something I have to tell you,' she
id, her voice barely more than a whisper.

Mal didn't appear to have heard. He stood up and
ok three restless paces, then spun back to face her,
hipped his cap off his head and slapped it against his
igh. 'Damn, she's ruined everything! I don't
iderstand how you can sit there and take this so
lmly.'

Abbie drew a deep breath and tried again. 'I realise
u're angry, but——'

'That had to be the understatement of the year,' he
uttered. 'Thanks to that publicity-hungry bitch, some
vo-bit reporter has scooped your story!'

He smacked the cap against his leg again, apparently
1aware that Abbie was gaping at him in stupified
tonishment.

'What did you say?' she managed to get out when
e'd recovered from her initial shock.

Mal frowned at her as if he suspected she was being
liberately dense. 'I said that some two-bit reporter has
ooped your story. That's what you call it, isn't it?
nyway, you know what I mean. And you don't even
em to *care*!' He planted his hands on his hips and
owered at her. 'Dammit, Abigail, do you love me or
ɔt?'

Abbie's mouth opened, but no sound came out. She
lt strangely light-headed. Mal started to blur around
e edges, and then suddenly there were two of him.
es,' she whispered. 'I think . . . I'm going to faint.'

The last thing she remembered seeing was Mal—bc
of him—dropping the cap and lunging forward. The la
thing she remembered hearing was his alarmed voi
calling her name. Not Abigal, but *'Abbie!'*

When she came to he was there, leaning over her, I
face a taut, anxious mask as he gently wiped a dar
washcloth across her brow.

'Are you OK?' he asked with gruff concern.

Abbie nodded. 'I think so.' She started to sit up and
quickly slid a supporting arm around her.

'Are you sure?' he said as he wedged the pillo
between her back and the headboard of the bed.

She nodded again. 'I'm OK, really.'

Mal watched the colour return to her cheeks ar
evidently decided that she wasn't going to faint again,
least not in the next few seconds. He left her to go to t
desk, where he poured Coke into the plastic glasses.

'I don't mind admitting you threw quite a scare in
me,' he said. He sat beside her gingerly, as if he w
afraid of jostling her, and handed her one of the glass
'I've never seen anybody faint before.' His bro
suddenly furrowed in concern. 'D'you think you mig
be pregnant?'

Abbie spat Coke down the front of her shirt. M
jumped back up and grabbed a handful of napkins fro
the desk. She gave him an afflicted look as she snatch
one from him and ineffectually tried to blot the liqu
before it could leave a stain. 'Are you trying to make r
faint again?'

'Well, it's possible,' he defended. 'At least, I assume
is. From what you told me about your sex life, I dou
that you're on the pill, and I didn't use——'

'All right!' she interrupted. If she'd been pale a coup
of minutes ago, now her entire body was suffused wi
embarrassed colour. 'There's no need to enumerate

he methods of birth control we *didn't* use.'

'So it is possible,' Mal said. The hint of smugness in his voice earned him a resentful frown.

'I suppose so,' Abbie muttered. 'Though I think it's more likely that I fainted because of a combination of hunger, exhaustion and plain old-fashioned shock.'

Mal's lashes suddenly dropped, but not before she saw the wickedly amused gleam in his eyes. 'Poor baby,' he murmured with mock sympathy as he got up and made another trip to the desk. He collected the pizza and the bottles of Coke and brought them back to the bed. 'Are you strong enough to feed yourself?'

Abbie let a theatrical sigh and a put-upon look serve as answer. She waited until his mouth was stuffed with pizza and then said, 'Damn you, Garrett,' in an extremely annoyed tone.

Mal grinned, swallowed and bit off another large hunk of pizza.

'You knew!'

'That you were a reporter?' he said calmly between bites. 'Of course I knew.'

'Freelance journalist,' she corrected peevishly. 'When did you find out?'

'I suspected you were the lady reporter I'd been hearing about as soon as you walked up to me in the hotel bar——'

'*Bull*oney!' she put in and was blithely ignored.

'—but I was willing to give you the benefit of the doubt, until you started spinning that incredible yarn about how your boyfriend left you high and dry at some fleabag motel.'

Abbie's teeth cleanly sliced off a section of pizza. 'What was so incredible about that story?' she demanded. 'I thought it was pretty good, considering how little time I had to compose it.'

Mal smiled indulgently and leaned over to wipe a dab
of tomato sauce from her upper lip with his napkin. 'For
one thing, I couldn't see you putting up with a boyfriend
who was as big a jerk as you made Larry out to be,' he
drawled. 'And for another, no man in his right mind
would have driven off and left you stranded in the
middle of cowboy country—not if he ever hoped to see
you again.'

'OK, so you didn't believe my story,' she muttered
irritably. 'Still, you couldn't have known for sure that I
was a writer.'

'True,' he admitted. 'But then I got all those phone
calls while you and Deke were in town collecting your
things.'

Abbie had trouble swallowing the pizza in her mouth.
'What phone calls?' she asked, not at all sure she wanted
to hear the answer.

'Well, first Eddie Carmichael called. He's the waiter at
the hotel bar. After the three of us left, his boss clued
him in about the pretty lady he'd been gossiping with,
and Eddie decided he should warn me that you were a
big-city reporter.'

Abbie closed her eyes and groaned.

'Then Iris Murphy called. Iris operates the hotel
switchboard. She thought I should know that you'd just
phoned a newspaper in Washington and offered them a
story about me.'

Her eyes flew open. 'She listened in on my call! That's
illegal!'

Mal shrugged. 'You were an outsider, darlin'. And
after what happened with Roxie . . . well, I guess they
were all trying to protect me from myself. The Garrett
men do have a reputation for making fools of themselves
over beautiful women.'

Abbie's mouth quirked in a wry smile. 'I'll probably

wish I hadn't asked, but did anyone else call you from the hotel?'

'Just Myrl Norris, the desk clerk. Cousin Lewis called from home. I believe you've met Lewis—he owns the hardware store,' he explained with a grin. 'He saw you leave the hotel with Deke as he was locking up for the night. And of course Deke found out who you were from Rafe Collier and hurried down to the garage to tell me as soon as he got back.'

Abbie slumped back against the pillows with a dejected sigh. 'I might as well have hung up a giant Press card around my neck.' She frowned as she replaced a half-eaten slice of pizza in the box. 'But if you knew who I was all along, why did you let me drive the Shelby?'

'You're a smart lady,' Mal drawled. He moved the pizza box to the floor and, while he was bent over, took off his shoes and socks. 'You should be able to figure it out.'

Abbie automatically scooted over to make room for him on the bed, taking one of the pillows with her. 'You *wanted* Press coverage of the race?' She made it a question, and a rather sceptical one at that.

He stood, smiling down at her as he stripped off his shirt and unfastened his jeans. 'See, I knew you could do it.'

Abbie was completely baffled, and it showed. 'Then what was all that business at Glady's—"Reporters are no better than scavengers. No, they're worse . . . they're parasites," ' she quoted. 'Do you have any idea how that made me feel?'

'Guilty?' Mal guessed as he kicked his jeans aside and joined her on the bed. He reached for her, but Abbie shoved his hands away.

'That was the whole idea, wasn't it?' she accused. 'You *intended* to make me feel guilty.'

Mal reached out again. This time he didn't let her push him away, wrapping his arms around her and throwing one long leg over hers to hold her still.

'Get off!' Abbie ordered.

'No,' he refused calmly. 'Not until you've heard me
out. It's true, I did hope you'd feel just a little bit guilty,
but that wasn't the primary reason I said those things. I
wanted it to be *your* story, you little dimwit. If I hadn't
come on so strong, Roxie would have dug in her heels
and refused to back down. Her editor friend would have
had daily reports splashed all over the front page of *his*
paper and the race would have been old news by the time
we got to Washington.'

Abbie felt about two inches tall. 'Oh,' she muttered.

'No, don't you feel ashamed?' he asked in the sexy
murmur that made her toes curl.

She ducked her head to hide a smile. 'Yes. But I already
felt ashamed.'

Mal's lips caressed her temple. 'I know. You've been
absolutely miserable for the last two days, wanting to tell
me the truth but afraid that if you did I'd blow my stack
and drop out of the race.'

'And fall straight into Roxanne's clutches,' she added as
her arms crept around his neck.

'There was never any chance of that.' He eased a little
to one side, just enough to slip a hand between them and
start unbuttoning her shirt. 'I knew what she had in mind
when she suggested the race, but I also knew she didn't
have a prayer of winning. That's why I agreed to the
terms of the bet. I suspected she might try to
cheat—falsify her log or something—but it didn't occur to
me that she might be so desperate that she'd risk
sabotaging the Shelby,' he admitted ruefully.

'When I found out Tony was going to be her driver, I
figured we were safe. Tony Ferris wouldn't lie or cheat for
Roxie or anybody else. I thought just having him along
would keep her honest. I should have known better.'

One of his hands tugged her shirt-tail free of her jeans while the other slipped inside the shirt and found her breast. Abbie released a soft sigh of pleasure. 'I don't want to talk about Roxanne Winston.' Her fingers slid into his hair and she urged him down, capturing his mouth for a hungry kiss.

'Neither do I,' he murmured against her cheek as he laid a string of baby kisses to her ear. 'Let's talk about the dynamite story you're going to write about my engine, instead.'

Abbie's eyes drifted shut. She combed her fingers through his hair, luxuriating in the cool, silky feel of it against her skin. 'Let's not,' she said with a languorous smile. 'Anyway, my story isn't going to be about your engine or the race.'

'What?'

Suddenly Mal was looming over her, an arm braced on either side of her. He didn't look happy.

'What do you mean, you're not writing about my engine?' He sounded as if she'd deliberately insulted him. Abbie hastily squelched a smile.

'I mean that I've decided not to focus on the engine,' she told him patiently. 'I'll mention it, of course, but my story's going to be about Malachi Garrett, the man.'

'The hell it is!' he retorted. 'You're not wasting valuable column inches on me, when you could be writing about one of the most important technological advances of the last fifty years. My God, Abigail, you could win the Pulitzer for this story. I *want* you to write about my engine. Why the hell do you think I brought you along, anyway?'

Abbie was unmoved by his agitated harangue. 'I thought it was because you'd fallen madly in love with me,' she murmured as her palms skimmed his chest, drifted over his ribcage and settled lightly on his waist.

He frowned at her. 'Don't try to distract me, Abigail.'

'Would I do that?' she asked innocently. Her right hand moved down and around, so that her fingers could trace a series of intricate designs on the back of his thigh.

'It won't work,' he warned sternly.

Abbie smiled. His body was offering contradictory evidence.

'I wasn't in love with you when I decided to let you drive the Shelby.'

She affected a disappointed pout. 'You weren't?' Her left hand began to imitate the movements of the right.

'No,' he said firmly, then relented with a crooked smile. 'I was well on the way, but trying like hell to convince myself that what I felt was nothing more than common, ordinary lust. Speaking of which . . .' He reached back to capture both her hands and moved them to his chest.

'There, that's better,' he muttered, ignoring the arch look she gave him. 'Now, settle down and pay attention. You have to write about the engine. It's important, Abbie, and not just because it's my design. If we don't stop squandering our natural resources, there won't be anything left for future generations. We have to start concentrating our energies and our talents on conservation instead of reckless consumption, and the key to turning things around is going to be public awareness. That means media coverage, and lots of it.'

Abbie's heart swelled with pride and love. Before she met him, she had heard Malachi Garrett described as an eccentric recluse, a misanthrope, a man so protective of his privacy that he had little or no use for the rest of humanity. She decided it was time someone introduced the world to the real Malachi Garrett—the man who was liked and respected by everyone who knew him; the man who worried about preserving the earth's resources for people who hadn't been born yet.

'OK,' she said huskily. 'You've convinced me. I'll write about your engine . . . if you'll agree to let me do a piece about you when that story's finished.'

He hesitated, his eyes narrowing as he considered the proposition. 'I'm not not a very interesting person, you know.'

'I disagree,' Abbie said with a smile. 'I think you're utterly fascinating.'

One shaggy brow rose a sceptical centimetre. 'Even if you wrote it, you probably wouldn't be able to sell it anywhere.'

'I'll take my chances.'

A shrewd gleam entered his eyes. 'The kind of article you have in mind . . . how long would it take to put together?'

'Several months, at least,' she said solemnly. 'First I'd have to do very thorough research—interview your friends and relatives, the people you went to school with, that kind of thing.'

'I've attended a lot of schools, and I have more relatives than a dog has fleas,' Mal cautioned. 'Assuming you devoted all your time and energy to tracking everybody down, it could take a year or more. How and where would you live while you were doing all this research?"

Abbie rubbed a lazy finger over the dark stubble on his jaw. 'I have a small nest egg. I could probably afford an inexpensive apartment, or maybe an older house. Of course it would help if I could find a roommate to share the expenses.'

'And the housework?' he suggested as he finally got around to easing her out of his shirt.

'Defintely. Somebody with nice long arms and legs.'

Mal tossed the shirt over his shoulder with a grin. 'To reach the cobwebs in the corners?'

'And the house moss under the beds,' she added as she wriggled out of her jeans.

He gathered her to him with a loving smile. 'You're in luck, Abigail Prudence. I happen to know someone who meets your requirements. He's a very nice reformed chauvinist who just recently decided that he needs a roommate.'

'You don't say,' Abbie murmured as she wrapped herself around him. 'Anyone I know?'

'You're looking at him,' he said with another devilish grin. 'There's just one tiny little condition.' His head suddenly descended, his hot breath caressing her breast in the instant before his tongue sent flames licking through her veins. 'I'd have to insist that you sign a long-term lease. Would that present a problem?'

Abbie pretended to give the question serious consideration; no mean feat when his hands and mouth were lighting fires up and down her body.

'That depends,' she said breathlessly. 'How long are we talking about, approximately?'

Mal pulled himself up to face her. His velvet brown eyes glowed with tenderness and love. 'At least thirty or forty years,' he murmured, no longer teasing but utterly serious. Hopeful. Vulnerable. Abbie's breath caught audibly as her throat constricted with emotion. 'Too long?' he asked, suddenly uncertain.

'No!' She shook her head adamantly. 'Definitely not too long. When do you think I could move in?'

The creases between his brows disappeared. 'How long would it take you to drive from Washington to Oklahoma?' he countered huskily as his mouth found hers.

'Two days,' Abbie murmured against his lips.

In fact, it took three times that long. They made a lot of stops on the way.

Harlequin Presents.

Coming Next Month

Available in October wherever paperback books are sold, or through Harlequin Reader Service.

In the U.S.
901 Fuhrmann Blvd
P.O. Box 1397
Buffalo, N.Y. 14240-1397

In Canada
P.O. Box 603
Fort Erie, Ontario
L2A 5X3

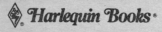
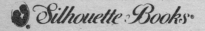